CRONE OF MYSTIC SPARKS

MYRTLEWOOD CRONES 4

IRIS BEAGLEHOLE

I

DELIA

The days followed a serene, rhythmic pattern. Each morning was heralded by the sound of a bell, its clear, resonant tones stirring the sisters from their slumber, a gentle call to the day's duties and rituals.

Delia stretched and dressed in the simple white robes before joining the sisters to eat a simple breakfast of porridge in the dining hall. She then made her way, serenely, out to the gardens enjoying the vibrant colours and fragrant scents from the multitude of flowers and herbs. There, she tended the rosemary, lavender, and thyme, each breath she took a reminder of the glorious harmony of nature.

As she tended the gardens, Delia found a deep peace in the slow, methodical work. Her hands moved with grace, caressing the leaves and stems as she pruned and weeded. Around her, the sisters worked in quiet harmony, each absorbed in their tasks.

"You seem to have a natural touch with the herbs," Elara commented as she worked beside Delia.

Delia smiled, her hands pausing in their work. "It is so peaceful here, in the rhythm of the garden. It's calming and healing."

Elara nodded, her eyes reflecting the tranquillity of the Clochar. "The garden has always been a place of refuge for us. The plants listen, and in their way, they speak."

Despite the tranquillity, a nagging sensation lingered at the back of Delia's mind, a feeling that there was something she had forgotten, a task left unfinished or a path not taken.

She could not quite put her finger on what it was – a whisper of discord amidst the clarity of the Clochar, a shadow on the edge of her serene existence here.

One evening, as the sisters gathered for their communal meal, Delia voiced her thoughts to Elara. "I feel at peace here, yet there's something...something I can't quite remember. It's like a dream I'm trying to recall."

Elara considered her words, then replied softly, "Perhaps it is the path you have walked before coming here. The Clochar is a sanctuary. Every sister here has a journey beyond these walls, a story that is theirs alone."

Delia nodded. "I had a life before this place. I know that much, but I struggle to recall the details, like a distant dream."

Elara put a sympathetic hand on her shoulder. "I feel the same way, though I believe I've lived here for most of my life. I used to struggle, to resist, but now I have embraced the harmony of this place and I no longer have to worry. Perhaps you will do the same?"

Delia smiled. "Perhaps I will."

The Clochar was indeed a sanctuary, a place of healing and respite, yet deep down, the discordant notes became deeper and more resonant, like a novice violin player amid a skilled symphony orchestra.

That evening, bathed in the ethereal glow of moonlight, the Clochar was transformed, yet again, into a realm of silver and shadows.

The sisters, dressed in their longer flowing white robes, congregated at the temple of the goddess. They gathered in a circle, their voices rising in a sacred chant that resonated with the very heartbeat of the earth.

The ceremony drew to a close and Delia stepped out of the temple, feeling a deep sense of peace and connection. The disharmony she'd experienced earlier had been soothed to the point of vanishing. One of the elders, dressed in a robe of silver, who had helped to lead the ceremony, approached Delia, her presence commanding yet gentle.

"How are you finding your time here?" the elder asked.

Delia paused, the tranquillity of the night momentarily giving way to confusion. "Where exactly am I?"

The elder offered a kind smile and extended her hand. "I am Gwyneth, one of the elder sisters. You are within the heart of the Clochar of the Veiled Sisterhood."

At these words, a fleeting memory flashed through Delia's mind – a woman with a kind, innocent face and white hair plaited neatly.

"Mathilda?" Delia said, the name escaping her lips almost involuntarily. "Isn't this where Mathilda lives? Where is she?"

Gwyneth's expression changed subtly, a shadow of sadness passing over her features.

She cast her eyes to the ground before looking back at Delia. "Mathilda is indeed part of our sisterhood, but she is away at the moment. She's occupied with an important task, one that requires her full attention and dedication."

Delia sensed the weight behind Gwyneth's words, a heaviness. There was a story there that Delia could only guess at.

Gwyneth placed a reassuring hand on Delia's shoulder. "She is where she needs to be, as are you. The Clochar is a place of healing and reflection. While you are here, let its peace envelop you."

Delia nodded, accepting Gwyneth's words, yet the mention of Mathilda stirred something within her – a connection to her past and the journey that had led her here.

"The moon teaches us about cycles, about the ebb and flow of life and emotions. Just like her, we too are ever-changing, ever-evolving," Gwyneth said, her gaze reflecting the moonlight.

Around them, the night air was filled with the residue of the ritual – the scent of burning herbs lingered, mixing with the earthy aroma of the Clochar's gardens.

The chants of the sisters still echoed in Delia's ears, a haunting melody.

Delia felt a twinge of unease. The Clochar, for all its serenity, held secrets.

Here, she found peace and tranquillity, yet something was amiss.

As she walked back to her sleeping quarters, a mysterious

symbol etched on the temple wall caught her eye – an intricate spiral pulsing under the moonlight. She didn't know what it meant, but the discordant resonance returned to her. A flash of Mathilda's face appeared in her mind again. She searched behind this memory, hoping for more, but all she could find were the peaceful days spent here, at the Clochar.

She knew she'd had a life before all this, but why couldn't she remember it?

2
MARJIE

Marjie shivered despite the warmth of the fire crackling in Ingrid's hut. Outside, the night was alive with the sounds of the forest – the distant hoot of an owl, the rustle of leaves in the gentle breeze, while the air inside was scented with aromatic mugwort tea, mingling with the sharper scent of sherry.

Marjie took a sip of her tea, feeling her brow furrowing in worry. "Where do you think Delia could have gone? No matter which scrying charm I try I can't locate her. Do you think she's alright?"

Agatha set down her sherry glass. "I wish I knew. One moment she was there, the next...vanished! It must have been that blasted Order of Crimson. Surely they could block your scrying with all their ridiculous magic. All signs point to them, don't you think?"

Ingrid raised her eyes from the flames. "I'm not sure. Something tells me that was a ploy – a red herring – a clever trick to set us on the wrong path."

Agatha wrinkled her nose in suspicion. "Who could it be then?"

Ingrid let out a long slow sigh. "My mind keeps returning to my sister. She was up to something. I'm sure of it. The Sisterhood went around handing out those charms." She motioned to the small leather pouch sitting on the mantelpiece. "I haven't quite deduced its magical nature yet – not exactly – but something about Mathilda's behaviour, and the illusions, makes me think they set everything up to kidnap us, and managed to nab Delia."

Agatha scoffed. "Ridiculous!" Then, catching a rather sharp glance from Ingrid, she added, "I mean that the Sisterhood is ridiculous if they think they'll be getting away with that."

Marjie chuckled dryly. "Well, that's a relief, actually. I'd rather she be sipping tea with a bunch of cloistered sisters than in the clutches of the Order."

"Tea? With the Sisterhood, it's probably more like moon-water or some other mystical concoction," Agatha quipped.

"Do you really think they'd be so devious, Ingrid?" Marjie asked, nervousness creeping back into her voice. "I could try scrying for her again, but I'm afraid whoever took Delia has put something in place to block my magic. If she is indeed with the sisterhood, she's probably okay, isn't she? They're not evil like the Order."

"I believe, at their core, the Veiled Sisterhood are zealots," Ingrid said cautiously. "They may seem all love-and-light—"

"That's why I can't stand them, personally," said Agatha.

"A bunch of robed goody-goody's getting involved where they're not wanted."

"But at least they are 'goodies' and not 'baddies'," Marjie added.

"I wish it were that simple," said Ingrid. "Certainly compared to the Order, they're much less barbaric, but that does not make them less dangerous overall. Remember that many of the worst atrocities committed by human beings have been supposedly to create a better world without care for the consequences."

Marjie shivered again and huddled a bit closer to the hearth.

Ingrid picked up the sherry bottle, pouring a small measure into her cup. "If Delia is with the Sisterhood, she will be safe enough – for now – but we cannot let them get away with their plan, whatever it is."

"I bet they think they're so smart." Agatha grimaced and then smiled. "They probably think we'll be on a rampage – going after the Order to get our friend back."

"They won't expect us to work out it's them..." Marjie added optimistically.

"If it actually is them," Agatha said. "I need more evidence because unlike you lot I don't go on blind faith and hunches."

Marjie sighed. "So much for your brush with intuition, Agatha."

Ingrid frowned. "Regardless of whether my hunches are bogus or not, we must figure out a way to get Delia back. If the Sisterhood have her, they're not going to let her go easily –

they'll use her to lure us all in. I'm sure they're after the power of the Crones, and for that they need the lot of us."

Marjie nodded in agreement. "Yes, and we may well need extra help and more information. It's not like we can just call her on her mobile phone." She lowered her gaze. "I already tried three times."

Ingrid shrugged. "The Sisterhood don't allow that kind of technology."

Agatha snorted. "Imagine if they did. We could just give them a bell. 'Hello, yes, we'd like one Delia back, please. No, we don't need gift wrapping'."

Their laughter filled the hut, tinged with anxiety.

Agatha, her brows knitted in worry, broke the silence. "How did Delia end up with us – up there on that cloud island, anyway? Where did that portal come from? Surely she hasn't mastered such advanced magic."

Marjie, her eyes reflecting the flickering flames, responded thoughtfully. "I believe Delia had help. In fact, I believe that rogue tracker was with her before she joined us on the island."

Agatha coughed on her sherry. "The bloke she turfed out of the pub?" She raised an eyebrow. "What was he doing with Delia?"

Marjie blushed and waved the question away with an exaggerated shrug.

Ingrid got up to stir the embers with a poker, adding another log of wood. "If the tracker was indeed with her," she said, "it's possible he may have had something to do with her sudden disappearance."

The idea that the tracker might have kidnapped Delia sent a ripple of concern through the room.

Agatha looked perplexed. “But why?”

Marjie took a slow sip of her tea, her gaze lost in the flames. She didn’t want to reveal what she knew of Delia’s newly rather intimate relationship with the tracker – which she’d caught a glimpse of while scrying – and regardless of their ‘closeness’ Marjie knew that he could still be working for the Order while seducing a Crone.

Ingrid shrugged. “Perhaps I was wrong in implicating the Sisterhood. It could be the Order using illusion magic to throw us off their track – as soon as that dragon disappeared I doubted whether it was really them. Perhaps that was their goal all along. Now I’ve gone and confused myself...”

“What would the tracker gain from taking Delia?” Marjie asked.

“It’s not what he gains, but what the Order gains,” Ingrid said. “Delia’s connection to us and her knowledge could be valuable to them.”

Marjie shuddered. The hut now felt like a shelter against an unseen storm brewing in the darkness of the forest.

Ingrid sat back, her expression resolute. “We need to find her, and quickly. If the Order is involved, Delia would be in imminent danger.”

They sat in silence for a moment, lost in their own thoughts, the only sounds the fire’s gentle crackling and the distant call of a night owl.

The front door creaked open and Mephistos slinked in.

“Well, look at what we have here. A gathering of crones

without their little firestarter," he said, his voice smooth with a hint of mockery.

Ingrid eyed him with irritation and caution. "Spare us the theatrics, Mephistos. What do you want?"

Mephistos let out a low, rumbling purr, clearly enjoying being the centre of attention.

Agatha watched him with suspicion. "What brings you here, demon?"

Marjie couldn't help but be fond of the sleek black feline. *He might be a demon, but if you like cats you can't help but be under their spell,* she mused, smiling warmly at the creature and resisting the urge to reach out and scratch him behind the ears.

Mephistos settled himself comfortably near the fire, his tail curling around his body. "I bring news," he said, his voice a low, smooth purr. "The Order...they have been delving into something dark, something dangerous."

Agatha rolled her eyes. "So what's new?"

Marjie leaned forward. "What kind of dark and dangerous?"

Mephistos's eyes narrowed, reflecting the flames. "A fundamental shift in their magic. Have you not sensed it? They are tampering with forces that should be left alone. Powers that could threaten the very fabric of our world."

Agatha sighed. "Dark magic threatening the world. It must be Tuesday."

Ingrid, who had been silently listening, ignored Agatha and focused on Mephistos. "Do you suppose this shift in their magic could be related to Delia's disappearance?"

"Ah...yes." Mephistos yawned and stretched. "You managed to lose the newcomer, didn't you?"

Ingrid glared at him.

"It is possible," Mephistos added. "The Order's ambition knows no bounds, and with this new power, they are more dangerous than ever."

The crones exchanged worried glances. Marjie bit her lower lip, anxiously. The threat of the Order now seemed more immediate and sinister than any concerns they'd had about the Sisterhood.

Agatha picked up her sherry glass and took a big gulp. "If what you say is true, then we must act quickly. We can't let the Order gain any more ground."

Marjie bolstered herself against the sombre and anxious mood. "We need to find Delia. Whether she's with the Order or not, she's important."

Ingrid nodded in agreement. "We'll need a plan, and we'll need to be cautious. Mephistos, can you gather more information?"

The black cat's eyes glinted. "I'm not some servant messenger, you know. I'm an ancient god – there was a time when I was worshipped for my great power and dashing good looks."

Agatha scoffed. "Yeah, yeah. Now you're a cute wee kitty. But where are you even getting this information from? Why come to us now with a vague threat at all?"

Mephistos narrowed his eyes at her. "I'll have you know that I've been using this sleek and nimble form to sneak around the very compound of the Order. It's tense there – the atmosphere charged with fear. The leadership has become tyrannical."

"Can you get us inside?" Marjie asked eagerly.

Mephistos cleared his throat. "I haven't actually made my way inside."

Agatha let out a cynical guffaw.

"The protections are rather elaborate," Mephistos admitted. "Even for me, but I know where it is. I've been tailing the guards and listening to their gossip. It seems the Crimson Shepherd has staged a coup against the Order's elders and unleashed magic such as they've never seen in their lifetimes."

"At least that's more specific and believable," Agatha conceded. "Delia's ex-husband is a nasty piece of work. I'd love to teach him a lesson."

"Is Delia there?" Marjie asked, her heart thrumming with concern. "We can't seem to figure out where she is."

"Not to my knowledge," said Mephistos. "If she's been captured by the Order they're keeping it secret – even from their own guards."

"We need more information," Marjie said urgently. "Please?"

"And what do I get in return?" Mephistos purred.

"Ingrid won't unleash her dragon hound on you?" Agatha suggested.

"Don't antagonise him," Marjie scolded before turning back to the sleek feline creature who was now preening himself. "You want to be released, don't you? From your physical form – you want to return to the underworld."

Mephistos yawned again. "I suppose I do. Most days."

"Of course you do," said Ingrid. "Otherwise why would you be going to so much trouble to spy for us and give us this information."

Mephistos gave her a pointed look. "Oh, very well. Yes, I'm dying to get out of here. And to achieve that, I shall do what I can to help you. But be warned, the shadows grow deeper, and the Order's eyes are everywhere."

As Mephistos sauntered back out into the night, the crones sat in silence. His cocky demeanour might have been infuriating, but the gravity of his message was not lost on them. The threat of the Order, now seemingly more dangerous than ever, loomed over them, and the urgency to find Delia and counter whatever plans the Order had in motion became even more pressing.

In the flickering light of the fire, Marjie's face was etched with concern. "I bet that dragon in the sky was a ruse by the Order to snatch Delia. It's just the sort of trick they would pull."

Ingrid looked over at Marjie, a thoughtful expression on her face. "Marjie, while your theory could hold water, we need more evidence before we can say for certain."

Marjie, not easily dissuaded, huffed, "Evidence, schmevidence! When have we ever had the luxury of evidence? Half the time, we get by on pure luck!"

Agatha rolled her eyes. "Well, that would explain some of your magical mishaps – not to mention that recyclable toilet paper business you tried to start."

Marjie blushed a little. "That was a long time ago."

Ingrid smirked at the exchange but then grew serious.

"Regardless, we need to consider all possibilities. The Order, the sisterhood, or something else entirely...Delia's disappearance could be linked to any of them."

Marjie leaned forward, her eyes reflecting the fire's glow. "If the Order has her, then Delia is in danger. We know what they're capable of."

Agatha sighed, pouring herself some more sherry. "Yes, and we also know that jumping headfirst into a situation without a plan is Marjie's specialty."

Ingrid, still gazing into the fire, seemed to be lost in thought, as if she was holding something back. "There's more at play here than we know. I can feel it," she murmured.

Marjie nodded. "Then let's uncover it. We're crones, not cowards."

As the night deepened and the fire burned lower, the crones sat together, each lost in her thoughts.

Marjie stared into the flickering flames, her mind racing with scenarios and possibilities. From her perspective, everything pointed towards the Order's involvement.

They're cunning, always a step ahead, she thought, her worry for Delia gnawing at her. The memory of Delia's laughter, her sharp wit, and the strength she brought to their circle made Marjie's heart ache.

Agatha said dryly, "Marjie, you look like you're plotting a siege on the Order's headquarters. Please tell me we're not going to sneak into their dungeon by dawn."

Marjie smiled wryly. "A dungeon? Oh, Agatha, you underestimate us. We'd at least make it to the tower room before getting caught."

Ingrid, still gazing into the fire, added with a hint of amusement, “And who would be leading the charge? You, Marjie, with your wooden spoon as a lance?”

Marjie chuckled. “Why not? I’ve always fancied myself a bit of a knight in shining armour. Or in this case, a crone in a well-worn cloak.”

Her attempt at humour did little to mask the undercurrent of fear that ran through her thoughts. Delia’s disappearance wasn’t just a missing piece of their shared strength, it was also the dread of a friend gone missing. In her heart, Marjie issued a silent plea to all the powers that existed, all the gods and goddesses that might aid them to please see Delia returned safely.

3
DECLAN

Under the cover of night, Declan approached Thorn Manor, the tower looming before him like an ancient sentinel. The building's very walls pulsated with a power that was formidable and arcane while simultaneously being somehow warm and inviting.

He paused, taking a moment to steel himself; he knew the gravity of what he was about to do.

To save Delia, I must seek the aid of those she trusts.

With a deep breath, Declan rapped sharply on the manor's heavy wooden door. It swung open, and Marjie appeared. As her eyes landed on him her expression was both surprised and suspicious in equal measure.

"I'm here as a friend," Declan said. "Or, if you do not trust my friendship, at least trust that we both care about Delia."

He was expecting far more resistance. In fact, he'd prepared magical protections, hidden in the palm of his hand in case of attack, but Marjie surprised him.

She assessed him for a moment, then looked around him into the dark night. "You'd better come in."

Inside, Declan was struck by the warmth that contrasted with the night's chill. He declined Marjie's offer of a drink; time was of the essence.

The grandeur of Thorn Manor was not lost on him. The high ceilings adorned with intricate plasterwork, the walls lined with bookshelves filled with ancient tomes, and the large windows draped with heavy curtains spoke of a legacy as timeless as his own.

In the living room, the crackle of the fire filled the silence between them as they sat down.

Marjie observed Declan with a critical eye as she led him to a pair of armchairs by the fire. "Why should we trust you?" she asked.

"Because I have nowhere else to turn," he admitted, his voice tinged with a vulnerability that he rarely allowed himself to express. "And because Delia...she deserves freedom."

Marjie's gaze was expectant. "What do you know?"

Declan met her eyes. "I know where Delia is," he confessed. "But the signal is faint."

Marjie relaxed slightly, her posture easing as she took in his words. "Tell me about this faint signal you've found."

Declan described the ethereal thread of magic he had detected. "It's not like my usual response to tracking. It's more like a whisper, fragile and fleeting, and it's so faint, I fear it won't last. I've tried to get to her, but I can't maintain a portal to her location for long. That's why I've come to you. I need your help, especially since I...I can't go through it myself."

Marjie's eyes narrowed. "And why is that?"

Declan hesitated. "Because I'm a...man," he said finally. "The portal won't permit me."

"Does that mean she's with the Sisterhood after all?" Marjie said, her eyes both sad and hopeful. She slumped into her chair with relief. "Better there than with the Order, I suppose."

Declan nodded solemnly. "The magic of the Veiled Sisterhood is strong. I do not know much about them, but they seem more gentle than the Order of Crimson, at least. I believe she will be safe, for now, but the fact that she was kidnapped at all disturbs me."

"As it does me and the other Crones," said Marjie.

Declan leaned slowly towards her. "Do you trust me enough to help me – or to let me help you?"

Marjie's expression tightened. "If you want my trust, then tell me your story. How did you get tangled up with the Order? And how did you manage to break free?"

He shifted uncomfortably. Centuries of keeping his secrets weighed on him, but he knew better than to let people know too much. Even Delia couldn't know the truth about his long existence. "I was under contract," he said, choosing the words carefully. "Years ago, I was bound to my work and blessed with magic. Since then, I've taken on any work that came my way, even though at times I've been tormented by the things I've had to do."

"So the Order contracted you to find Delia," Marjie said.

"That much I could have guessed. But there's more, isn't there? A lot more..."

"Believe me when I say it's a long story," Declan admitted. "But I found a way out," he said, his voice barely above a whisper. "I don't know how, but Delia freed me..."

"And you love her," Marjie said. It wasn't a question. She simply knew. Declan understood this about the water crone – she was intuitive beyond measure, and it was no coincidence he'd gone to her to plead his case. He did not have to answer her. She saw into his heart and she knew what love he harboured there.

Marjie studied him for a long moment before nodding slowly. "Then it seems we have a common goal. We must find Delia."

"Yes, we must," he agreed. And for a moment, in the shared silence that followed, an unspoken alliance was formed.

4

INGRID

Ingrid sat alone in her forest hut, the smell of hearty stew bubbling on the fire filling the small space with a comforting aroma. She cradled a wooden bowl in her hands, savouring the warmth it lent to her fingers.

Her peaceful evening was abruptly interrupted by the sound of urgent knocking. With a sigh, Ingrid placed her bowl on the rough-hewn table and went to the door. Swinging it open, she found Marjie and Agatha standing there looking both concerned and determined.

Ingrid frowned. "What brings you two here unannounced? I was enjoying my stew and my solitude."

Marjie stepped forward with a warm smile. "My apologies for coming so late and without warning, but we have rather urgent news, and you're going to want to hear it."

Ingrid stood aside to usher her in.

Agatha followed, her usual scepticism evident in her furrowed brow.

Ingrid closed the door with a thud, her annoyance fading at the obvious gravity of the situation. “What news?”

“Declan visited me,” Marjie said. Then, when Ingrid raised an eyebrow, she explained. “The tracker, you remember.”

“What did he want?” Ingrid asked.

Marjie beamed at them. “He’s found Delia, or at least, he knows where she is.”

Agatha snorted. “And of course Marjie believed him. The man’s a tracker for the Order!”

Ingrid, however, paused as something within her sparked instinctively. Her stew sat neglected as the three Crones settled in by the fire.

“Where does he say she is?” Ingrid asked.

Marjie picked a small bottle out of her handbag and poured three small glasses of it, then handed them around before speaking. “He claims she’s with the Sisterhood, in their Clochar.”

Ingrid's eyes narrowed as she took a sip of the beverage that turned out to be some kind of spiced mead. “I wouldn’t put it past them, like I told you. The Sisterhood is not beyond doing nefarious things if they believe it’s for the greater good. They’re zealots, the lot of them, including my own sister.”

Marjie nodded, her gaze flicking between Ingrid and Agatha. “I can’t explain exactly how, but I trust him, and I’m asking you to trust me.”

Agatha downed her mead then held up her cup for more. “And what if he sends us straight into the Order’s clutches?”

"He's no longer under the Order's employ," Marjie said. "He's been trying to break free of them for a long time, and now he finally has."

"A likely story," Agatha grumbled.

Ingrid looked from Marjie to Agatha and back again. The warmth from the fire did little to dispel the cold dread that began to settle in her chest at the thought of walking into a trap.

Marjie's face was resolute. "He will not betray us to the Order, he's even willing to take an oath to prove it. There isn't time for doubt. We must move fast and get Delia back."

Agatha huffed, her disbelief clear, but Ingrid could see the concern etched deep in her features.

"This had better not be a wild goose chase, Marjie," Ingrid said, a touch of concern creeping into her voice. "Or a trap."

Marjie simply held her gaze, her plea silent but intense.

Ingrid looked down at her untouched stew, the rich scents now a background note compared with the urgent tension in the room. "Then we act swiftly. And the tracker..." She trailed off, her mistrust of the man still a bitter taste in her mouth. "He'd best be telling the truth."

Agatha, leaning against the rough stone mantelpiece, looked dreadfully unimpressed. "So, we're now to place our trust in a man who's been hounding us at the behest of the Order? Splendid!"

"Oh, come off it, Agatha," said Marjie. "You act as though you've never taken a risk before. What about that time you tried to enchant your own cauldron to cook your dinner?"

Ingrid allowed herself a small smile, as Agatha spluttered a barrage of insults in response, before conceding. “Oh fine! But if this goes awry, Marjie, I’ll be holding you responsible.”

Marjie met her eyes, a steely glint in her own. “I take full responsibility if it means you’ll get out of my way.”

The urgency in Marjie's voice was hard to ignore, even for someone as stoic as Ingrid.

Ingrid cleared her throat authoritatively. "Agatha, for once, can you drop the snark? We must focus."

Agatha's expression softened, and she gave a conceding nod. "Fine.”

Ingrid let out a slow breath, her gaze drifting towards the window where the night pressed against the glass, the forest a black canvas hiding all manner of secrets. She served her uninvited guests bowls of stew and the room lapsed into silence as they ate. She looked at the empty chair that should have held Delia's laughing form; the absence felt like a missing tooth.

“I don’t trust this tracker,” Agatha reiterated.

“Well, that’s too bad,” Marjie said. “Because he’s the best chance we have. He can cast portals with a speed and skill unlike any witch I’ve ever met.”

Ingrid shook her head. “Portals can’t breach the Clochar, surely.”

Marjie reached out and put her hand on Ingrid’s forearm. “Declan’s portals are different. His magic is unlike anything I’ve encountered before – ancient and powerful. In fact, he’s already tried to portal there, and while he could not get through himself, he believes that with our help, he will be able to hold a gateway just long enough for us to sneak in. He’s coming back tomorrow night to help.”

Ingrid, her eyes widening in disbelief, almost sloshed stew from her bowl. “Here? To my sacred space?” she asked, the very idea seeming to violate the sanctity of her home.

“No, not here,” Marjie clarified quickly, seeing Ingrid’s protective stance. “To Thorn Manor, then. There’s more space and something tells me we’re going to need it.”

Ingrid gave Marjie a withering look. “I may have ventured out on a pilgrimage or two, but do I really have to go into *town*?”

Marjie chuckled. “I’m sorry, Ingrid. But it seems we need you to set foot outside of your forest if we're going to get Delia back.”

Ingrid frowned. The idea of venturing into Myrtlewood was as appealing as wading through a swamp – which was another thing she’d been contemplating recently. An adventure in the wilderness was one thing, but a foray into town was something she almost never forced herself to endure. “I suppose desperate times call for desperate measures.”

5
AGATHA

Agatha had barely settled into the familiar embrace of her library, the smell of leather and parchment enveloping her like an old friend, when an unexpected knock sounded, rapping sharply against the front door. With a sense of trepidation, she strode to answer it, pulling open the heavy wood to reveal Covvey's weathered face.

"Covvey, what on earth?" Agatha said.

The lines etched in his forehead softened slightly.

"What are you doing here?" she asked.

"It's freezing out here, Agatha. Took your sweet time, didn't you?"

Agatha swatted at him. "Oh, come in out of the cold and tell me what's going on." She beckoned, leading him into the sanctuary of her beloved library, the walls and shelves lined with the wisdom of the ages. The room, usually a cocoon of solitude, felt suddenly vulnerable.

"You know, in all the years I've known you, Agatha, I've never been in here," Covvey remarked, his eyes scanning the towering shelves cautiously.

Agatha shrugged, her hands slipping into the pockets of her robe. "You're not in the habit of making house calls, it seems. So what's changed?" she inquired, pouring him a glass of whiskey before pouring herself a sherry.

There was only one chair by the fire, but Covvey retrieved the matching armchair from under a pile of books that Agatha had yet to sort.

The silence was thick and uncomfortable. Agatha stared into the fire, waiting for Covvey to speak. He hadn't responded to her question, so she decided she'd better ask again and again until he gave her a straight answer.

"So, Covvey, are you going to sit there in silence all night, or are you going to tell me why you're here?"

Covvey made a grumbling sound. "It's nuffink," he mumbled.

"Nothing?" Agatha scoffed. "You expect me to believe you came all this way for nothing?"

Covvey grumbled again before finally admitting, "I can smell danger, you know. Your lot is in trouble."

Agatha's lips pressed into a thin line. "We don't need your nose in our business, Covvey."

Technically, everything to do with the legendary Elemental Crones of Myrtlewood was still a secret, and the less others knew the better – for their own safety. "It's nothing you need to concern yourself with," said Agatha.

Covvey, however, was not deterred. "I know about the

legends of the crones, and I've got this feeling something of that nature is coming to pass."

Agatha grimaced. "I don't trust feelings," she stated flatly.

"Well, perhaps it's worth giving them a try, for once," Covvey challenged, giving her a meaningful look that sent an uncharacteristic blush creeping up Agatha's cheeks.

She shifted awkwardly, the flush of colour on her face so at odds with her usual composed demeanour. "Look, I'm not supposed to talk about it," she snapped. "And perhaps you should be on your way if that's all you came here for."

"You might not want help, but you damn well need it," Covvey said, remaining seated, his presence a steady anchor in the room. He regarded her with a look that was both understanding and challenging. Agatha, despite her words, made no move to usher him out.

"You don't have to talk about it," Covvey insisted. "I know enough already."

Covvey held her gaze, the warmth from the fire doing little to thaw the sudden chill between them. "Agatha, you're a strong woman and I've always respected your boundaries, but this is different. You're in the middle of something big, and I want to offer my help. You know I have no family of my own."

Agatha thought of what she knew of Covvey's past. He'd confided in her once, after far too many whiskeys, that his mother had abandoned him when he was just a young pup. His father had been a violent man, and Covvey had run away as a young teen, fleeing from beatings. He'd made his way, finding a job as a blacksmith's apprentice, but he'd always been a lone wolf. She looked away; it was a sad story and the weight of their impending mission to rescue Delia was also pressing down on her. Covvey's concern, while unwelcome, was not unfounded. It was certainly a dangerous situation, and this unexpected visit reminded her that the Crone's actions affected more than just themselves.

Agatha pondered whether perhaps it was time to let others in on the big secret. At first, nothing to do with the Myrtlewood Crones had been certain, and keeping things hushed up made sense as they discovered and struggled to wield their new powers. The dangers too, were unknown, and she had thought it safer to keep other people out of it. Now, however, the dangers were becoming more and more obvious. Perhaps it was time to trust in the strength that allies like Covvey could offer. But for now, she remained silent.

The fire's glow seemed to accentuate the intensity in Covvey's eyes as he faced Agatha. "I've just come here to help," he repeated stubbornly. "Enough with the secrets, Agatha. This is bigger than just you."

Agatha's thoughts drifted back to Delia. A sharp bitterness edged her voice as she looked directly at Covvey. "Do you know Delia has gone missing?" she asked sternly. "Is that why you're here? You fancy her. I can tell."

Covvey shook his head in frustration. "Is that why you've been distant lately?" he asked, amused. "You think I'm after your new friend."

Agatha let out a heavy sigh, her defences wavering. "It wouldn't be the first time," she grumbled, recalling the women he'd gone after over the years. She could not offer him that kind of companionship, it wasn't in her nature, and Agatha was generally content with her nature even if her ridiculous emotions sometimes got the better of her.

Covvey's expression softened. "I didn't know she was missing," he admitted. "I came here to help you...but of course, I'll help her — all of you. I just need to take action somehow. I can't sit around while the town's in peril. I'm stubborn, you know."

Agatha narrowed her eyes. No one could out-stubborn her – well, except for Ingrid and occasionally Marjie and Delia on their better days. She held his gaze and remained resolute. "There's no use in that. We have to help ourselves. That's all there is to it."

Covvey leaned forward, his hands clasped tightly as if to anchor his words. "No," he said firmly, his gaze never leaving hers. "You're in trouble, Aggie, I can feel it. I've been holding back for long enough. I know you're strong and that's why I've left you to it until now, but I've been catching strange scents on the wind. Something big is coming, and I'm here to offer any assistance I can give."

Agatha's facade of stubborn indifference faltered for a moment. She glanced away, her gaze landing on the spines of ancient books, guardians of secrets and knowledge, as if seeking reassurance from them.

Returning her attention to Covvey, Agatha's expression tightened. "Covvey, your concern is noted," she said grudgingly. "But don't think for a second I'll change my stance."

Covvey shook his head. "Even the toughest crone needs an ally now and then. And I've got a bad feeling about what's coming."

Agatha sighed. "I don't trust feelings as we've already covered, Covvey. I trust what I can see touch, record, and analyse."

"Perhaps," Covvey said gently, reaching out to place his hand upon her own, "it's time to trust in more than just yourself. I'm here, Aggie. And I'm not going anywhere."

Agatha did not recoil at his touch as she'd anticipated. Of course, they'd been friends for a long time, and surely Covvey knew that she did not possess a romantic bone in her body, so he wasn't here to seduce her...surely. Yet here he was, presenting her with the most uncomfortably earnest conversation they'd ever shared. It was quite frankly infuriating!

The fire crackled between them and Agatha blew out a disgruntled breath. Covvey's presence was an annoying comfort she didn't know she needed and his words of warning had a ring of truth to them.

"Alright, Covvey," she finally conceded. "Fine, you can tag along. But don't expect a warm welcome. We're meeting tomorrow night at Thorn Manor. You're a powerful wolf. The others might not like it, but I know we'll be safer with your support."

Covvey saluted her in a gesture of gratitude, downing his whiskey in one smooth motion. He stood, casting a long look at Agatha before turning to leave.

The door closed behind him with a soft click, leaving Agatha alone with her thoughts.

Reaching for the air dragon pendant at her neck, she whispered, "We have work to do."

6
ELAMINA

Elamina Bracewell Thorn stood as her aunt entered the drawing room. Sabrina Bracewell, with her dignified yet austere appearance, carried an air of authority that demanded respect. She regarded Elamina with a critical gaze.

"Elamina, I must speak with you about the impostor," Sabrina began, her voice carrying the familiar tone of disapproval.

Elamina braced herself. "If you're referring to Delia, I haven't been able to dig up any dirt on her like you requested. All I can ascertain is that she is, as she said, new to the magical world and that she is indeed part of our family."

Sabrina's nostrils flared in irritation. "That may be so, but you must understand, my dear, associating with her is not appropriate. It raises questions about our discernment. Not that that will be an issue for the time being."

Elamina raised an eyebrow. "Delia may be related, Aunt

Sabrina, but she is hardly our kind of 'people'. I assure you, my interactions with her are nothing more than necessary politeness."

Sabrina nodded, her expression still critical.

The truth was, Elamina quite liked Delia Spark, despite only meeting her twice before. She was sharp and confident, and lacking the airs her family tended to put on. It was refreshing. But of course she held all this back from her aunt. Sabrina wasn't one for being contradicted, and Elamina tended to pick her battles with strategy in mind. In this family of sharks, any vulnerability was like blood in the water.

As Sabrina continued to express her disapproval of Delia, Elamina nodded along, giving the impression of agreement. "Of course, Aunt Sabrina, I understand the importance of maintaining our family's reputation."

She didn't want to mention it, particularly in present company, however, Elamina couldn't help but admire Delia's unapologetic authenticity. It was a quality that she, in the confines of her social circle, often yearned for but could seldom express.

Sabrina leaned forward, her voice lowering conspiratorially. "And speaking of choices, you'll be relieved to know the situation with that impostor, Delia, has been...handled. The threat has been neutralised."

This was what Elamina had been waiting for, more clues as to her aunt's cagey communications surrounding the matter of Delia Spark. 'Neutralised' sounded ominous. Masking her concern with a polite smile, she risked a question. "How exactly has the threat been neutralised?"

Sabrina let out a short laugh that sounded like a bark, surprising both of them. “It’s nothing to worry about, Elamina. And certainly nothing that would concern the magical authorities with which you so gracelessly associate yourself with.”

Elamina couldn’t help but frown. Her aunt despised political ambition, particularly in women, but this wasn’t a time to start arguments.

“Aunt Sabrina,” Elamina said, as calmly and politely as she could manage. “I appreciate that you wouldn’t want the authorities involved with anything involving the family, so may I have your word that no harm has come to...the impostor?”

Sabrina pouted for a moment and then regained her composure. “No harm has come to her, as far as I can tell. And it wasn’t my doing, I’ll have you know. Delia, it seems, is more than capable of getting herself into trouble, and some old associates of mine are ensuring she’s no longer a risk to herself or others.”

Elamina inhaled slowly. “Very well. Then there will be nothing to report, and the reputation of the family can remain untarnished.”

Elamina maintained her composure until she’d left the drawing room, but outside her facade of calm wavered in concern for Delia. Without wasting a moment, she summoned a driver and gave the instruction to proceed to Myrtlewood without delay.

Arriving at Delia's house, Elamina knocked briskly, hoping her aunt had been mistaken and that Delia would open the door. Rumours ran rife in the magical community, after all, and there was a reasonable chance Sabrina had received incorrect information.

The door opened, revealing an unfamiliar woman around Delia's age with a silver bob and a quizzical expression.

"Who are you?" Elamina asked, trying to mask her surprise.

The woman raised an eyebrow. "Excuse me?" She seemed taken aback, but then her features softened into a grin. "Silvery hair, arranged to perfection, an elaborate tailored outfit, and an expression that could freeze the River Thames...Ah, you must be Elamina. I'm Kitty, Delia's best friend."

Relief momentarily washed over Elamina. "Where is she?"

Kitty's smile faded, replaced by a look of genuine worry. "I only wish I knew." Her words hung in the air, and Elamina felt a cold dread settle over her.

7

MARJIE

Marjie sat at the old oak table in the cosy kitchen of Thorn Manor, sharing a light supper with her dear friends Rosemary and Athena. A pot of herbal tea steamed gently in the centre of the table, its soothing aroma mingling with the scent of fresh bread.

"I'll have visitors later tonight," Marjie casually mentioned as she buttered a slice of bread. "Agatha and another friend, Ingrid. They're coming for...a special magical reason."

Rosemary leaned forward. "Oh, Marjie, you and your secrets. I do wish you'd tell me what's really going on." Her tone was light, but there was a hint of genuine longing to be included.

Marjie chuckled, shaking her head. "I can't, Rosemary. You know that. It's not up to me."

Athena laughed. "Mum, you hate to be left out of a good secret," she teased.

Rosemary playfully nudged her daughter. "Well, who wouldn't? Especially when it's something as exciting as Marjie's mysterious magical meetings."

Marjie felt a sense of warmth that went beyond the temperature of the room as she smiled mischievously at her chosen family. "I promise, if I could tell you, I would. But this is...complicated."

Rosemary sighed, reaching for a piece of cheese. "Complicated seems to be the theme of our lives."

Athena grinned. "It's like a secret society that Marjie's part of – I'm sure of it."

Rosemary laughed. "I've had quite enough of those! Although any society with Agatha in it is bound to be terrifying."

Marjie laughed, the sound echoing around the kitchen. "You're not wrong. Agatha is a force to be reckoned with!"

Marjie glanced at the clock. It was still early, but soon the calm of the evening would give way to urgency.

As if in response to her thoughts, there was a knock on the door. "They're early," she muttered under her breath.

Marjie's expression shifted from surprise to mild concern as she opened the door to see – not the other crones, but Kitty standing there. She opened the door wider to let her in, only to reveal none other than Rosemary's snooty cousin, Elamina, resplendent in a silver suit.

Elamina's entrance was like a gust of cold wind, contrasting sharply with the warmth of the kitchen. Her eyes, sharp and discerning, immediately found Rosemary. There was a hint of disdain in her eyes.

Elamina paused. Her gaze swept over them. “I suppose you're all wondering why I'm here,” she said, with a touch of haughtiness as everyone's attention turned to her.

Rosemary’s eyes were wide in shock, but she managed a strained smile. "Elamina, this is a surprise.”

Elamina glanced briefly at Athena, a softness momentarily touching her features, before turning her attention back to Marjie.

"I heard a rumour about Delia," Elamina began, her tone measured. "I needed to see if it was true."

Marjie’s heart fluttered in fear. “What rumour is this?”

Rosemary raised an eyebrow as she glared at Elamina. "And why should you care?"

Elamina's expression hardened. "Because she's my cousin," she stated matter-of-factly.

"I know that," Rosemary replied, her tone dry. "But I’m also your cousin and I hardly think you'd come to my rescue, despite the fact that we knew each other as children."

Elamina's lips curled into a faint, condescending smile. "I'm sure you couldn't begin to fathom my motivations at any point," she retorted. "But I won't hold it against you."

Athena rolled her eyes in exasperation. "Stop it, you two," she interjected. "Clearly there's something serious going on here that’s not helped by your childish rivalry."

Rosemary frowned but returned her attention to Marjie. "I assume whatever has happened to your new friend Delia is related to all the secrets you’ve been keeping.”

Marjie nodded. “I’m afraid so.”

Rosemary sighed. “I'm tired of being kept in the dark," she

declared, her frustration evident. "I demand to know the whole story, especially as others arrive who also seem to know what's been going on."

Marjie sensed that the time for secrecy had passed. She gathered her thoughts, preparing to share the truth about the Myrtlewood Crones, but before she could find the words, Kitty interrupted.

“Look, I’m sorry to barge in like this,” Kitty said, her eyes imploring Marjie. “But I need to know where Delia is. I thought she was with you. But it seems you’re back. So where is she?”

Marjie released a heavy sigh, though she was somewhat relieved to be distracted before revealing secrets she’d promised not to tell.

“I’m afraid we’re just about to find out,” Marjie said. She briefly explained the situation of Delia’s disappearance, the words spilling out with a sense of urgency.

“She’s been taken somewhere?” Kitty’s asked, concerned. “I mean, I’m glad she didn’t plummet to her doom, but where on earth...”

“Her tracker friend has a theory,” Marjie interjected, attempting to offer some semblance of hope.

Kitty’s expression lightened slightly, a smirk playing at the corners of her mouth. “Oh, you mean the hot cowboy?” she asked.

Marjie couldn’t help but smile. “I do believe so,” she replied, a mild blush warming her cheeks. “As a matter of fact, he and Delia seemed to get a lot closer on our last adventure, but I’ll not share any details.”

Kitty shook her head, her smirk widening. “I’ll have to grill

Delia for all the interesting details," she said wryly before becoming more serious again. "I only hope you can get her back soon."

Rosemary and Athena, who had been listening intently, exchanged worried glances.

Marjie patted Kitty on the shoulder. "We'll do everything in our power to bring her back."

Kitty nodded. "Thank you, Marjie. I know if anyone can bring her back, it's you and your lot."

Just then, another knock sounded at the door. Marjie turned towards the sound, a sense of anticipation filling the room. The night's work was about to begin.

Moments later, the tracker stepped into the warm kitchen, his presence immediately altering the room's dynamics. "This is Declan," Marjie said. "He's here to help with...our current situation."

Kitty's eyes lit up mischievously as she took in Declan's rugged appearance. "Well, hello there," she greeted him, her voice dripping with flirtatious undertones as she extended a hand. "I remember you from the pub and I've heard a lot about you..."

Declan, clearly unaccustomed to such attention, looked slightly mortified but managed a polite nod.

Kitty laughed off his discomfort. "Oh, don't mind me. That's just how I am with any tall, dark, and handsome stranger," she said with a wink.

Declan cleared his throat. "We need to get to work," he said. "Where are the other crones?"

The word 'crones' caught Rosemary's attention. "Crones?"

she echoed, her curiosity piqued. “Now, Marjie, I know this is supposed to be secret, but you really must tell us now, especially as everyone else seems to know.”

Marjie hesitated, caught between the confidentiality of her circle and the inquisitive eyes of her friends. Before she could formulate a response, another knock at the door interrupted them. “Ah, that will be them,” she said, a note of relief in her voice as she walked past Rosemary and Athena, their expressions ripe with curiosity.

Marjie quirked an eyebrow as she greeted Agatha standing at the doorstep, but she wasn’t alone. The sight of Covvey accompanying Agatha was unexpected, to say the least.

Marjie began to protest, but Agatha cut her off.

"Don’t you start," Agatha said sternly, stepping into the light of the doorway.

Marjie couldn’t help but throw up her hands in exasperation. “What happened to keeping secrets?” she asked in frustration.

Agatha was quick to defend herself. “I didn’t tell him,” she argued, a hint of defensiveness in her posture. “He already guessed. Besides, in a small town like this, nothing stays secret for long.”

Marjie sighed. “I suppose you’d better come in, then,” she conceded, stepping aside to let them enter.

Covvey, a gentleman despite his gruffness, tipped his hat to Marjie as he crossed the threshold.

He growled at the sight of the tracker.

Declan didn’t even flinch.

“He was the one Delia kicked out of the pub,” Covvey said, bristling.

“That time has passed,” Marjie assured the aggravated wolf shifter. “Settle down or you’ll create more of a mess than we’re already in. We have more important things to deal with.”

“But where’s Ingrid?” Agatha inquired, looking past them through the front door.

“Here I am,” came a voice from the darkness. Marjie peered out to see Ingrid tethering her goat cart.

Marjie held the door open as Ingrid made her way inside. She glanced back at the cosy kitchen, where Rosemary, Athena, and Kitty were waiting with evident curiosity.

“It seems every man and his biscuit knows about our secrets now! This is going to be too hard to keep from Rosemary and Athena,” she muttered. “We’d better tell them.”

Moments later, settled in the living room of Thorn Manor, Marjie gave a brief overview of the secrets surrounding the Crones, with frequent interjections from Agatha.

“I think we’ve heard enough backstory,” said Kitty. “Where is Delia and how are we going to get her back?”

“Apparently, she’s in the Clochar of the Veiled Sisterhood, where I grew up,” Ingrid said. “And it’s not an easy place to get into unannounced.”

Marjie looked towards Declan. "Apparently, he can portal us there.”

Covvey bristled again. "How do you know you can trust him?" he asked, his gaze fixed on Declan. "He could be portalling you anywhere."

Marjie put her hands on her hips. "I know because my gut says so." Marjie replied, casting a stern look at Agatha who – in deference to the gravity of the situation – didn't even take the opportunity to quip about Marjie's gut.

Kitty, her earlier flirtations forgotten, rounded on Declan with a piercing look. "As far as I know, you've been tracking my best friend for weeks and handing information to that horrible Order of Crimson. What's changed?"

Declan met her gaze with a grave expression. "Everything," he said simply. "I can't explain it all now, but I will put every ounce of strength and magic I have into rescuing Delia and still, I can't do it alone." He looked around at the crones. "I need your help."

Covvey glowered at him. "But why do you need help? You say you can cast a portal there. If you really want her rescued, why not just cast a portal stealthily and do it yourself?"

"I suspect it's because I'm a man," he said in frustration. "Like I said before."

Ingrid sighed. "Of course. No man can set foot inside the Clochar. The magical protections are far too strong for that."

Declan nodded. "I can barely hold the portal open, let alone go through. But if I put all my energy into keeping it open, and perhaps with some additional power anyone can lend me, I can see to it that you three" —he gestured to Marjie, Agatha, and Ingrid—"can slip in, at least."

Elamina stepped forward. "While I don't usually align myself with such...rustic methods, I must admit, this plan seems to have a certain...utility."

Marjie exchanged a look with Agatha and Ingrid.

"We'll do it," Marjie declared, her voice steady. "It's worth the risk if it means we can rescue Delia."

8
DECLAN

Declan's gaze swept over the eccentric gathering of witches as he stood silently in the corner of the living room. His tracker instincts compelled him to observe and catalogue every detail, every nuance.

Marjie, at this time, was the clear leader of this unique assembly. He sensed this was not usually the case, but her closeness to Delia, her determined demeanour, and the fact that she'd summoned people to gather this night, gave her the gravity of a sun around which everyone else orbited. He admired her ability to rally thc group with her soothing and energising words.

Then there was Agatha, the most acerbic sceptic among them, sitting rigidly. Her keen eyes missing nothing. She exuded an air of authority and no-nonsense practicality. Her distrust in him and her disbelief in the unproven was a challenge he would have to overcome.

Ingrid had an earthy, grounded presence that seemed to anchor the room. She was the most knowledgeable about the Clochar, yet she used her words sparingly. Ingrid struck him as someone deeply connected to the natural world, a woman whose wisdom was as vast as the forest she called home.

As he watched, Ingrid approached Marjie and Agatha, passing them small bundles tied with twine. Declan noticed that she too wore one around her neck. "These should protect us from the magic of the sisterhood, at least for a little while," Ingrid explained, her tone serious. "From what I know of it." She held up an extra bundle. "This one's for Delia. When we find her."

"Looks like we're all set for a witchy field trip," Marjie joked.

Agatha clutched at the bundle. "I swear, if I end up smelling like clary sage for the next week, I'm blaming you, Ingrid."

“It would be an improvement on your natural odour,” Ingrid shot back.

Marjie chuckled, trying to keep the mood light. "Think of it as aromatherapy, Agatha. Might help with those grumpy moods of yours."

Agatha shot Marjie a mock-stern look. "I'll have you know, my 'grumpy moods' are a vital part of my charm."

Ingrid laughed. "Indeed, they're what make you so endearing, Agatha."

Declan watched as Marjie and Agatha secured the bundles around their necks. Something about this reassured him. They were not unprepared. They were powerful, and Delia had the best chance of return with their help.

As for the others gathered around, it was evident that the Thorn witches, Rosemary and Athena, were powerful, as was Elamina, despite being rather haughty and aloof. Covvey was a protective wolf shifter, Declan knew that much from their brief interactions. His powers would not likely be useful, but he could stay as long as he didn't get in the way. Then there was Kitty, the only non-magical person among them. She was vulnerable, but so sassy that he didn't like his chances in trying to get her to leave for her own protection. Marjie had already tried twice – explaining the risks to her in getting too close to powerful magic – but she refused.

Declan drew his attention inwards as he mentally prepared himself for the tasks ahead. Opening and maintaining the portal to the Clochar would be a test of his endurance.

Declan felt the lead weight of the responsibility resting on his shoulders. It was an unfamiliar sensation. For so many centuries he'd only ever answered to himself and his employers, but now there was something personal at stake, someone indescribably precious.

He chastised himself internally for not being there to protect her, for letting her slip into danger.

Ingrid's stern voice broke through his thoughts. "Do you give us your word that this will work?" she asked, her eyes locked onto his, searching for any sign of deceit.

Declan met the gaze of each crone in turn, his expression earnest. "I will not deceive you," he assured them. "I'm sure I can get you there, but I cannot be sure of your safe return.

There are too many variables. I can wait for the count of say, twenty minutes, then cast a new portal to the same exact coordinates, so be ready."

Kitty interjected. "And if they miss the bus?"

Declan nodded, understanding the severity of the situation. "Then I'll try again and again. I will not give up, but if you've been captured and cannot reach the same location, it will be impossible."

"Then I'll go in after them," Rosemary said.

Athena agreed. "We can't abandon Marjie."

Marjie shrugged and responded calmly, "Let us cross that bridge if we ever come to it, dear. The Clochar is a place of peace so rest assured, if we are captured, we will be safe enough, even if getting back is tough. For now, let's get this party started!"

Marjie cleared the furniture to the sides of the room with a wave of her hand. "Declan?"

He nodded and stepped into the centre of the room, feeling all eyes upon him as he began the process of casting the portal.

His hands moved through the air with practiced precision, tracing intricate patterns that shimmered and glowed in the dim light of the room. The air around him grew charged with a deep blue energy.

"It's making the hairs on the back of my neck stand on end," Athena whispered.

"Mine too," said Kitty.

Declan paid them no attention. He had to focus. This portal was no ordinary one, and the magic of the Clochar was already fighting back; even as he tried to focus on Delia's location, he felt the magic slip away like butter on a hot pan.

Focus...

He drew more magic into the room, pulling it forth with his full concentration. The space before him began to warp and twist like the steam from a kettle.

Focus on Delia...

Gradually, the circular shape of the portal emerged, its edges flickering with light. Within the centre, a surface that appeared as black water under a crescent moon.

"Is it ready?" Marjie asked. "Can we go through?"

Declan nodded, bracing himself. "Quickly. I'll try to hold it for as long as I can, but it won't be for long." His voice strained with the effort as he glanced over to the grandfather clock nearby. "By the time the clock strikes eight I will endeavour to cast another portal, for your return."

As he strained against his own magic, he could feel the portal's pull; the chaotic vortex demanded his full attention and strength to keep stable.

"Alright," Marjie gave the rallying cry. "Crones to the rescue!"

They dashed through the portal, disappearing into the unknown. Declan watched them go, his heart heavy but his will unbroken. A moment later it closed, leaving the room in silence.

Declan stood there in bitter longing. He wished to follow them, to be by Delia's side, to ensure her safety with his own hands. But he was held back, relegated to the role of the caster, his powers limited to creating the gateway that would lead the crones to her. He could only hope that it would be enough.

9
DELIA

Delia wandered along the stone pathway between the herb garden beds, her hands dipping low to brush against the sage and rosemary bushes on her walk back from the moonlight chanting.

The harmonious notes of the melody still echoed in her mind, blending seamlessly with the night's serenity.

The gardens of the Clochar exuded aromatic fragrances, calming and invigorating her.

There was an undeniable sense of tranquillity in the air, a deep peace. Yet, as she pondered, Delia realised, yet again, that much of her past seemed like a distant fog, a storm cloud in an otherwise clear sky. She tried to grasp at the memories, but they slipped away like wisps of mist, elusive and intangible.

Reaching her bedchamber, Delia admired the simplicity and elegance of the room. The walls were adorned with a small painting of the mountains and delicate embroidery of a bouquet of spring roses. Her small window framed the view of the night sky. The glorious mother moon hung low amid the stars, its silvery light illuminating the room.

Under this light, Delia changed into her sleeping robes, a garment of soft, flowing linen. She moved gracefully, her movements unhurried and fluid, as if she were part of the night's gentle rhythm.

There was no need for a candle; the moon provided just enough light to see by. Everything was perfect. Delia gazed out the window, her eyes lingering on the moon as she settled into her bed. The chants from the temple still resonated within her, beaconing her toward sleep like a lullaby.

Just then, something caught her eye – a flicker of light. It was a subtle at first, a mere disturbance in the air, a ripple that grew more pronounced by the second.

The flicker transformed into a shimmering tear in the fabric of reality, right there in her tranquil room. It widened, the edges glowing with an ethereal blue light that pulsed and throbbed like a living thing. The air around bent and warped, and through this luminescent breach stepped three familiar figures who she instinctively knew by name, despite the foggy state of her memory.

Marjie, Ingrid, and Agatha stumbled into the room, their expressions reflecting both relief and urgency.

"Oh my dear, thank the gods we found you!" Marjie rushed forward to envelop Delia in a warm embrace.

Delia, surprised yet overjoyed, returned the hug with genuine happiness. "I'm so glad to see you all." She beamed, her voice filled with warmth.

"Great!" said Agatha. "That was far simpler than I feared. Now, let's get moving. Come on Delia."

Delia frowned. "Please, stay," she implored them. "The Clochar is a wonderful place. You'll all love it here."

Her friends, however, looked deeply concerned and confused at her words.

"They've muddled her mind," Ingrid grumbled, her brow furrowed in worry.

"There must be magic entrancing her," said Agatha, glancing around the room, as if seeking a source of enchantment.

Ingrid stepped forward. "It's powerful magic," she observed, her voice low and thoughtful. She seemed to taste the air, her eyes narrowing as she discerned the unseen threads of magic.

Marjie, Agatha, and Ingrid exchanged worried glances. Delia was sure there had been some misunderstanding. She continued to smile, knowing these women as true friends and hoping they, too, would find peace.

Ingrid's actions were swift and precise. She clutched something that hung around her neck. Delia's eyes came to rest on the bundle of herbs, reacting with further puzzlement. Was this some kind of talisman of protection?

"Here," Ingrid said as she reached into her pocket, brandishing another such charm, and quickly slipped it over Delia's head. The string of the charm settled around Delia's neck.

"I'm not sure how it will work on Delia," Ingrid muttered, "since the magic is already in full swing, but it might help diffuse things."

The tranquillity that had soothed Delia's mind began to ebb away, replaced by a growing sense of confusion and a greyness that clouded her thoughts.

Delia felt her body tense at the intrusion of discordant emotions into her serene world.

"No," she said, reaching up to tug at the charm.

Marjie stepped forward and stilled Delia's hand with her own. "My dear, remember who you are..."

Delia shook her head, disorientated.

"Remember your family," Marjie continued. "Gillian, and the grandchildren..."

Images swam into Delia's mind, faces and memories.

"Remember Kitty, and your real life," Marjie implored. "It's all waiting for you. You've been here in this dream, but it's time to wake up now. It's time to come back to us."

As Marjie's words filtered through, Delia felt a stirring of wakefulness. She braced herself against a sudden, splitting headache and groaned.

Just then, the sound of footsteps approached.

"Someone's coming," Agatha whispered.

Ingrid snapped to attention. "We must act quickly. Get her ready. Bar the door."

Marjie wrapped an arm around Delia's shoulder, offering support. Delia continued to groan as the charm around her neck glowed faintly.

"Hush now," said Marjie. "You'll feel better soon."

But as the footsteps grew louder, nearing the door, Delia noticed the doubt in Marjie's voice, just as she recognised the fighting stances Agatha and Ingrid had now taken.

Her calm had been shattered, and danger had crashed in upon her serene world.

10
COVVEY

Covvey stood watching, his senses on high alert. Declan's brows furrowed in concentration as he occupied the centre of the room, his hands moving in complex patterns, his focus entirely on the task of opening a second portal.

Covvey narrowed his eyes in suspicion as the air around Declan shimmered with a subtle fog magic, yet the portal refused to manifest.

Rosemary stood next to Covvey, arms crossed, watching. "Are you sure you can do this?" she asked, her voice tinged with doubt.

Athena, standing beside her mother, was the youngest in the room, yet her spirit was undeniably strong. "He has to try, Mum. Let him concentrate."

Rosemary shook her head. "There's too much at stake here. We can't lose them. There must be some way we can help."

Covvey nodded silently. Agatha, his oldest friend, was out

there, and he couldn't bear the thought of not doing everything in his power to bring her back.

Declan paused and slowly looked around the room. "There are powerful witches in this room," he said slowly.

"What's your point, man?" Covvey growled. "Can you open the second portal or can't you?"

Declan took a long slow breath. "The defences are stronger now. It's as though they've recognised my magic and responded to it, the way the body builds a defence against known threats."

"You want us to lend our magic?" Athena suggested. "Is that it?"

Elamina scoffed lightly. "*Lend* my magic?"

"You said you were going to help," Rosemary grumbled.

"It's one thing to help, using my magic in my own way, but powerful witches do not simply lend their magic for others to utilise as they see fit," Elamina protested. "Well, not unless one's cousins have almost brought about seasonal apocalypse."

Athena rolled her eyes. "Really, Elamina, do you have to bring that up right now?"

The house trembled slightly as if recalling the chaos of Yule, and Rosemary reached across to the mantelpiece to soothe it.

Declan cast his eyes down. "I understand why you may not trust me, but..."

"But there's too much risk in letting that stand in the way," said Rosemary, sharing a glance with her daughter. "We'll help."

Kitty frowned. “I wish I could do something, anything...to help.”

“Just being here will help,” Athena assured her. “Delia will be so happy to see you when she gets back.”

Declan looked from Rosemary and Athena to Elamina. “I need your magic,” he said. “I can’t do this alone. The Sisterhood’s magic has adapted, strengthened. We need all the power we can muster.”

Covvey, feeling the call to action, stepped forward. His wolf shifter magic was unique, adaptable, and he hoped it might make a difference. He locked eyes with Declan, a silent understanding passing between them.

Athena looked to Elamina, sensing her cousin’s hesitation. “This isn’t about us. It’s about Delia and the others, our friends, our family. We have to put aside our doubts, our pride, for them.”

Elamina, after a moment’s hesitation, rolled her eyes and stepped forward. “Never mention a word about my role in this...eccentric ritual – not to anyone.”

Rosemary laughed, but Athena elbowed her gently into silence.

As they gathered around Declan, each person began to channel their own magic, their energies merging into a collective force. Covvey focused on his shifter magic, tapping into the primal force that coursed through him. He may have hardly known his own family, but this force was who he was and where he came from. It was his feeling of belonging in the world, it was his very being, and he would channel it into this magic if it meant rescuing Agatha who had been the closest thing he'd known to family in many decades.

Declan's concentration intensified and the lines in his forehead deepened as he drew on the magical currents provided by those around him.

The air in the room thickened with the power of their combined energies. The portal magic, transformed from a mere shimmer, began to solidify, its edges flickering into existence.

Covvey felt the energy coursing through him, a wild and untamed force that contrasted with the more refined magics of the others. He pushed his power into the portal, his thoughts on Agatha, on the unbreakable bond he shared with the stubborn old witch. The thought of losing her, of failing her, fuelled his determination.

As the combined magic of the group poured into the portal, a strange, ethereal light began to seep into the room. It was like moonlight, but with an otherworldly quality that made the air ripple and warp. The light touched everything, casting long, wavering shadows against the walls of Thorn Manor.

The magic began to twist in the air, as if reality itself was bending. The light seemed to pulse with a life of its own, growing brighter. The beauty of it was mesmerising, yet beneath the surface, there lurked a sense of foreboding.

Covvey felt the strange magic like a tangible force, winding its way under his skin. It was beautiful yet ominous, like a tranquil poison seeping into his very being. His enhanced senses, usually a source of strength, now made him acutely aware of the magic's invasive touch.

The air crackled with energy, the very fabric of the room

seeming to vibrate. Covvey's heightened senses were overwhelmed by the barrage of stimuli, the magical energy almost too intense to bear. His instincts screamed at him to flee, to escape this unnatural phenomenon, but he stood his ground, determined to see this through.

Kitty, standing nearby, suddenly swayed. Her eyes glazed over, becoming blank and distant. With a soft sigh, she collapsed onto the sofa, her body limp, as if she had fallen into a deep trance.

Declan's voice cut through the tension, strained yet determined. "Keep going!" he shouted, his body trembling with the effort of maintaining the portal. "We're almost there!"

Covvey, fighting against the enchanting effects of the magic, focused on the task at hand. His body felt heavy, each movement requiring more effort than the last. He glanced at Rosemary and Athena, noticing their struggle to maintain their own focus amidst the growing chaos.

Rosemary's expression was one of fierce concentration, locked in a battle of wills against the encroaching magic.

Athena, though clearly affected, mirrored her mother's determination, her youthful resilience shining through.

Elamina, who had initially held herself apart with an air of superiority, now grappled visibly with the magic's influence. Her usual poised demeanour faltered, a rare look of uncertainty crossing her features. Yet, she too persevered, her pride driving her to resist the magic's tranquil allure.

The room swirled with energy and light, the portal's flickering edges growing more stable with each passing second.

The air vibrated with the power they were unleashing, a

storm of will converging on a single point. The tension was almost unbearable, pressing against them all.

Just as it seemed they could bear no more, the portal stabilised, its edges solidifying into a clear, steady gateway. The strange, moonlike light reached a crescendo before dimming, leaving them in the muted glow of the manor's lamps.

The portal, now a swirling vortex of light and shadow, pulsed with their combined magical efforts, but the tension in the room was almost unbearable. Each second felt like an eternity.

Covvey, his chest heaving with exertion, watched the portal. Hoping against hope that Agatha and the others would return safely. He couldn't lose her, not when they had come so far.

The portal now stood open with the swirling of light and shadow at its edges. The air around it warped and spun, the very atmosphere bending in its presence. New light from the portal spilled out into the room, touching everything with a surreal, otherworldly quality as if they were standing on the threshold of another world, a place where the normal rules of existence no longer applied.

11

INGRID

Ingrid stood in Delia's simple room, her senses acutely attuned to her surroundings. It had been years since she last set foot in this place that had once been her home. Now, as she stood there, a sense of unease gripped her.

Her eyes scanned the room, taking in the simplicity of the furnishings, the way the moonlight streamed through the window, casting long shadows.

The air felt different than it used to, charged with a magic that was both familiar and foreign. She clutched the bundle of herbs around her neck, grateful for the intuition she'd channelled while listening to the forest. She'd taken the charm Mathilda had given her and deciphered its magical properties, before creating the bundles designed to ward off the Sisterhood's magic. Even now, she could tell her protections were dispelling the thick magic in the air so that she and the other Crones would be safe from its spell, but for how long?

Approaching footsteps echoed through the corridor, a steady rhythm that set Ingrid's nerves on edge.

She braced herself for confrontation, aware that they were intruders in a place that did not welcome their presence.

Agatha checked her pocket watch. "We still have several minutes until the portal is supposed to return," she whispered.

Then came a soft knock at the door. "Sister Delia," a voice called out gently from the other side. The crones held their breath, remaining silent.

Ingrid's heart raced, her mind careening through possible scenarios.

She glanced at Marjie and Agatha, seeing the same determination in their eyes, ready to protect Delia and to face whatever or whoever was behind that door.

Ingrid's hand instinctively went to the bundle of protective herbs around her neck, again, seeking assurance. She felt the energy from the charm, a subtle vibration against her skin, reminding her of her own power.

The voice outside the door called again, a hint of concern in its tone. Ingrid knew they couldn't keep silent forever. Her eyes met Delia's, who seemed to be slowly coming back to herself, the confusion in her eyes giving way to clarity. Ingrid gave her a reassuring nod, but Delia stared back at her, dazed and silent.

Ingrid stepped forward, casting a simple locking charm to stop the door from opening. She prepared herself for the possibility of deception, of magic, of a fight.

Her many years away from the Clochar had taught her much, but now she was back, not as the naive youth she once was.

The door knob rattled and the voice outside became more determined. “Sister Delia. Please let me in. The elders summon you.”

Ingrid's heart raced. She could feel the urgency emanating from the voice in the hallway, a sister of the Clochar who was clearly determined to enter. The spell she had cast to hold the door was only a temporary solution, a fleeting barrier against the inevitable.

“I’m busy.” Agatha’s poor imitation of Delia’s voice was a desperate attempt to buy them more time, but Ingrid knew it was a weak ruse at best. “I’m just...changing.”

The voice outside grew louder and more insistent. “Let me in!”

Ingrid glanced at Marjie and Agatha. They were cornered.

“This portal better appear soon because we’re vastly outnumbered if the sisterhood all wake up and come after us,” she whispered.

Ingrid’s spell held the door fast, but the hammering sound that followed signalled their impending discovery. “Sister Delia! I must insist you open up right now or I’ll have to fetch the elders.”

The thought of Gwyneth, now an elder wrapped up in the business of the Clochar, struck a chord in Ingrid’s heart. Once, they had been closer than sisters, but now they stood on opposite sides of an unseen divide. The pang of longing merged with a sense of sorrow.

Ingrid knew they needed a plan, and quickly. The portal was their only hope, but until it appeared, they were trapped.

As the pounding on the door subsided and the sister’s footsteps echoed away down the corridor, Ingrid silently prepared for whatever confrontation lay ahead.

The room felt smaller, the air heavier, as the seconds ticked by.

Ingrid realised she had a message to convey. Her hands moved with haste as she scribbled a note.

Delia was staring blankly, still clearly under the influence of the Clochar's magic.

"She's not in her right mind," Agatha observed.

“No. We need to get her out of here, and fast," Ingrid agreed, her gaze flickering to the window.

A sound from the courtyard drew her attention. Peering out, Ingrid saw the elders of the Clochar sisters, including Gwyneth, leaving the temple, the messenger leading the way. The sight of Gwyneth stirred a flood of memories, but Ingrid pushed them aside. "I'd say we have about five minutes. Perhaps less.”

"This blasted portal is running late!" Agatha grumbled, her frustration evident.

"Not by much," Marjie reassured softly, her hand comforting Delia. "Don't you worry, Delia. We'll have you home and back to rights in no time."

Delia, her mind clearly still foggy, slumped against Marjie, who gently patted her head in a soothing gesture.

Ingrid glanced out the window once more, her heart skipping a beat as her eyes met Gwyneth's. The elder's gaze was piercing, filled with shock, recognition, and something else Ingrid couldn't quite place.

In that moment, a ripple of light shot through the air. The portal appeared, its swirling energy a beacon of hope.

Ingrid quickly cast the note onto Delia's bed, a final message left in their wake.

Without hesitation, the crones slipped back through the portal with Delia clinging between them.

As they disappeared into the swirling vortex, Ingrid took one last look back at the Clochar before leaving it behind for a second time.

12

GWYNETH

Gwyneth had been sitting in the tranquil temple, soaking in the energy from that evening's service, when she was interrupted.

Sister Breag's voice cut through. "Sister Gwyneth. We have a disturbance."

Gwyneth opened her eyes to see both the other elders, Breag and Franwen, standing solemnly before her.

"I've been watching the pool of illumination," Breag continued. "Someone has breached the Clochar."

Gwyneth's mind immediately went to the Crones. Who else would be powerful enough to attempt such a feat? "We must check on Delia."

"I've already sent a messenger," Sister Breag said.

Minutes later, the young sister sent to check on the captured Crone returned, her face etched with concern. "Sister

Delia will not respond, and the door to her chamber will not open," she reported, her voice trembling slightly.

"We must hurry," Sister Breag declared.

Gwyneth rose from her place, her heart heavy. The peaceful moonlight of the evening now seemed to cast ominous shadows across the grounds as they hurried through the herb gardens. A flood of memories washed over Gwyneth. She remembered the days when she and Ingrid, then just children, would play among these very herbs. They had tended to the plants together, their laughter mingling with the rustling leaves. They would pretend they were ancient healers or powerful witches, their imaginations turning the garden into a realm of magic and adventure.

With each step, Gwyneth's sense of unease grew.

Her gaze drifted towards Delia's sleeping chamber. The moonlight illuminated a face peering out from one of the windows. It wasn't the fire Crone, but the face was unmistakably familiar.

Ingrid...

There was no mistaking those eyes, even after all these years. A torrent of emotions surged through Gwyneth – surprise, confusion, and an aching nostalgia.

Before Gwyneth could process these thoughts further, Sister Breag's voice brought her back to the present. "We must keep moving," Breag urged, her tone insistent. She clearly had not caught sight of Ingrid.

Gwyneth quickened her pace, steeling herself for a confrontation.

She glanced back towards the window, but the fleeting glimpse of Ingrid's face receded into the shadows.

Gwyneth's heart raced as she reached the corridor outside Delia's room.

The door was barred with a simple spell, which took only a moment to break.

The elder sisters burst into Delia's chamber.

The room was empty.

The bedcoverings lay dishevelled. A note on the bed drew Gwyneth's attention. The handwriting was unmistakable – it was Ingrid's.

Gwyneth's hands trembled slightly as she picked it up. The message was concise, just two words, but they spoke volumes:

Back off.

Gwyneth stood there, holding the note; rage, confusion, and the sting of betrayal coursed through her.

Sisters Breag and Franwen stared at the note.

"What does it mean?" Franwen asked. "Where did the fire Crone go?"

Gwyneth was silent for a moment, contemplating how best to respond. "It means Ingrid was here," she finally said, her voice steady to keep from revealing her inner turmoil. "And she's involved in whatever happened to Delia."

"Outrageous!" said Sister Breag. "They stole her right from under our noses."

Gwyneth shook her head. "I feared they would retrieve her. She is one of them, after all."

"Do not speak out of turn, sister," said Franwen. "The

power of the Crones belongs to the Clochar. They all belong to us."

Gwyneth stiffened, awaiting judgement. Perhaps she had spoken too rashly.

Sister Breag merely bowed her head subtly. "You were right in fearing a breach in the Clochar," she said slowly. "I have never seen such a thing, in all my years, but it seems I was naïve to think our protections could withstand the power of the Crones."

"Let us return to the temple," said Franwen, with a touch of bitterness in her tone. "We must plan."

Gwyneth took one last look at the dishevelled bed, the note still clutched in her hand, knowing that the events of this night would have repercussions.

13
AGATHA

Agatha braced herself against the disorienting sensations. Tumbling through the portal, her world was a blur of uncomfortable light and shadow with no clear form. Just as the blur of confusion seemed it might go on forever, the hard wooden floor emerged and collected her. Along with the rest of the Crones, Agatha found herself in an ungainly pile, a tangle of limbs and magical energy.

Scrambling to her feet, Agatha quickly assessed the situation.

Covvcy looked drained, his usually formidable presence diminished, yet there was a steadfastness in his eyes that Agatha found reassuring. Declan was slumped against the wall, his energy clearly sapped, his breaths coming in laboured gasps.

Elamina, Rosemary, and Athena, however, were almost

radiant, their skin seeming to emit a faint glow. Agatha couldn't help but wonder at the strange turn of events. It was as if the magic from the portal had imbued them with some residual power.

She deduced the magic of the Sisterhood, designed to repel men, had taken its toll on Declan and Covvey. They both looked significantly weaker, not at all like their usual robust demeanours.

Delia was physically unharmed, the remnants of her trance falling away. Her eyes suddenly widened in alarm as she caught sight of Kitty, who lay motionless on the sofa, her eyes open but unseeing.

"Kitty!" Delia's voice was laced with panic as she crawled towards her friend.

Ingrid, taking in Kitty's state, tore open the herb bundle around her neck and looked around. "I need boiling water, quickly," she instructed.

"I'll get it!" Rosemary ran towards the kitchen.

Ingrid then turned to Athena. "And a saucepan, please?"

Athena followed her mother out of the room.

Meanwhile, Marjie rummaged through her handbag. She produced a small jar of ointment, which she gently applied to Kitty's temples. Her hands moved with experienced ease.

Delia, still on the floor, crept towards Kitty like a wounded cat, confused and worried.

"Marjie, what's in that ointment of yours?" Agatha asked.

"A bit of lavender, some chamomile, and a few other secrets," Marjie replied, her focus still on Kitty. "It should help calm her mind."

Agatha nodded, trusting Marjie's expertise for once.

Healing wasn't Agatha's forte. She watched, somewhat helplessly, as Ingrid began to concoct a herbal remedy in a saucepan of hot water.

Agatha's gaze shifted back to Covvey, noting the weariness etched on his face. He seemed to have aged years in the span of mere hours, the vitality that usually marked his presence now dimmed. A pang of concern washed over her for the stubborn old wolf, though she didn't want to show it.

As Ingrid steeped the herbs in the hot water, the aromatic scent wafted through the room. Ingrid took the saucepan over to the fireplace and held it above the flames. With a focused expression, she murmured a short incantation, her voice low.

Next, Ingrid poured the herbal concoction imbued with her magic carefully into a teacup.

"Here, prop her up a bit and hold this to her mouth, get her to drink," Ingrid instructed, passing the cup to Marjie.

Agatha frowned. "But we wore those herbal talismans to the Clochar," she pointed out. "What if it's infused with the very magic that's caused her to faint? Won't that make her worse?"

Ingrid smiled. "I'm counting on it," she said. "With my incantation, it should help her body to process the magic quickly, and hopefully before too much damage is done!"

Marjie propped Kitty up, then held the teacup gently to her lips.

"Here, Kitty, try to drink this," she coaxed.

Agatha watched with some scepticism. She trusted Ingrid's expertise, yet the uncertainty of the situation lingered. The magic they had encountered was unlike anything they had dealt with before, and its effects were unpredictable.

Delia began sobbing like a young child. “I did this to her... It’s all my fault.”

“Don’t be ridiculous,” said Agatha. “She insisted on being here. And besides, this is clearly the Sisterhood’s fault, not yours.”

Delia looked up at her. “But I...I was lost in a dream. I forgot her. I forgot everyone...How could I?”

Agatha hesitated, before patting Delia’s shoulder awkwardly. “That was their magic, and you’d be a fool to blame yourself for it. Now is not the time for wailing. Just focus on your friend now. Talk to her, reassure her. Encourage her to drink the damn magic tea!”

Delia wiped her tears away, regaining some composure. She turned back to her best friend. “Kitty. I’m here. I’m back. Everything’s okay. Thank you for trying to help me. I love you, now please drink the tea...please?”

Kitty’s eyes remained closed but her lips parted as Marjie gently pressed the teacup to them. Slowly, she sipped the herbal decoction.

Agatha couldn't help but feel a surge of hope. If anyone could reverse the effects of the Sisterhood's magic, it was Ingrid with her deep knowledge of herbs and ancient remedies and her lived experience of the Clochar.

The room was silent, save for the crackling of the fire. Every eye was fixed on Kitty, waiting for a sign of improvement.

Agatha's thoughts drifted back to Covvey and Declan. She

knew they would need attention as well, but for now, Kitty's recovery was the immediate priority.

This was the life of a crone, Agatha mused. A constant balancing act between the mystical and the mundane, the known and the unknown. The work never truly ended.

14

DELIA

Delia watched with bated breath as Marjie coaxed Kitty gently to drink. She still seemed unconscious, yet she slowly sipped Ingrid's magical tea, perhaps because Marjie's magic was coaxing her to do so.

The lingering effects of the Clochar's magic still clouded Delia's mind, but the sight of her best friend lying unconscious had cut through the haze like a sharp knife.

Delia's hands trembled as she reached out to touch Kitty's arm, the skin beneath her fingers feeling unnaturally cool. The scent of the herbal tea wafted through the air, mingling with the lingering traces of magic that clung to their clothes and skin. It was a strange combination, both comforting and unsettling, a reminder of the ordeal they had just endured.

"What happened to her?" she asked in a voice barely above a whisper.

Marjie's brow furrowed as she gently coaxed Kitty to drink

more of Ingrid's magical tea. “Kitty must have reacted badly to the magic.”

"I suspect it’s because she’s not protected by having any powers of her own," Ingrid explained, her voice heavy with concern. "The energies seeping through the portal overwhelmed her."

A wave of guilt crashed over Delia, the realisation that Kitty had put herself in harm's way for her sake settling like a lead weight in her stomach. She looked around the room, taking in the state of the others, her eyes widening as they landed on Declan.

He had clearly come to her rescue. His expertise in portal magic which impressed even Ingrid would have made all the difference in her rescue. Yet, the protections on the Clochar had clearly sapped him of energy; his usually vibrant presence was now muted and tired.

As Delia’s gaze lingered on him, their eyes met, and an electric connection shocked through Delia, the intensity of it momentarily stealing her breath. But she couldn't afford to be distracted, not when Kitty needed her.

She turned back to Kitty to see no apparent change, so instead of staring anxiously at her best friend she took in the others in the room.

Delia reached up and patted her best friend's shoulder. "Kitty, darling, I need you to come back to me. Please wake up." The words caught hoarsely in her throat, a desperate plea.

Memories of their shared past flashed through Delia's mind – the laughter, the tears, the countless moments of ridiculous fun that had forged their unbreakable bond. Kitty had always been there for her, a constant source of strength and support.

Seconds ticked by on the antique clock, louder for the silence in the room, each one feeling like an eternity. Still, there was no response.

Delia's vision blurred with the tears she tried to hold back, the room around her fading away until all she could see was Kitty's still form.

In a desperate attempt to rouse her friend, Delia leaned in close, her lips brushing against Kitty's ear.

"Kitty, if you don't come back to me, I'm going to terrorise you in the afterlife, you sneaky cow," she whispered.

Suddenly, Kitty coughed and spluttered, the tea Marjie had been coaxing her to drink dribbling down her chin.

A muffled moan escaped her lips. Delia held her breath, her eyes fixed on Kitty's face, searching for any flicker of movement or recognition.

Kitty turned her head, her eyes meeting Delia's with a glare that held a glimmer of her usual spirit. Delia's heart leapt into her throat, her shoulders softening as she breathed out a deep sigh of relief.

Kitty mumbled something inaudible.

"What is it?" Delia asked. "What are you trying to say?"

Kitty's lips twitched. "Not until after I haunt your mangy mortal existence first, Delia Spark," she croaked out.

A laugh bubbled up from Delia's chest, the knot of fear that had settled there finally beginning to loosen. If Kitty had the energy to joke, the worst must surely be behind them, at least, for now.

15
THE SHEPHERD

Father Benedict stood before the grand chamber, his heart pounding. At first the Elders had merely chastised him and then ignored him, sending him to his rooms to pray.

It had taken several days before they'd discovered the full extent of his betrayal, days in which he had strived to command the dark power burning within him, nights in which he'd restlessly tossed and turned in pain.

Benedict had heard whisperings of what had transpired. The guards of the Almighty had sensed a change, but no one had been brave enough to check. Finally, the Elders had sent a young novice to stand before the Almighty as punishment for sneaking a video game console into the compound. There, trembling before the door, the novice had discovered...nothing.

The Almighty had vanished from the chamber.

Now, Benedict was summoned to stand before the Elders again.

As he approached the heavy wooden doors, he could feel the weight of the Elders' judgement upon him. The air seemed to crackle with the tension of their fury.

Anticipation and trepidation coursed through his veins. He knew that the Elders would not take kindly to his actions, to the power he had claimed for himself. But he also knew that there was no turning back after what he'd done.

"Forgive me, Almighty," he whispered, pressing his palms into the door softly. "Forgive me for my hubris. Give me the strength to face what lies ahead, to defend the path that you have set before me."

He paused, his hand hovering over the ornate handle. He could hear the murmur of voices from within as the Elders discussed his fate. A slow smile crept across his face as he pushed open the heavy doors.

Taking a deep breath, he pushed open the doors. Elder Mordant's voice boomed across the circular room. "Father Benedict, you stand accused of a grave transgression. You have imbibed the Almighty's power, a forbidden act that threatens our very foundation."

Benedict met their gazes unflinchingly. "I have done what is necessary. The Sisterhood and the Crones grow stronger each day. We must adapt to meet these threats."

"Adapt?" Elder Firth sputtered. "You have violated our most sacred laws!"

"And yet, here I stand, blessed by the Almighty himself," Benedict retorted, a smile playing on his lips.

Elder Quill stepped forward, his finger shaking as he

pointed at Benedict. "You arrogant fool! Your actions could bring ruin upon us all!"

Benedict's expression hardened. "Chaos is already upon us. The enemy's power grows, and we must be prepared to meet it head-on."

As the Elders protested, a whisper filled Benedict's mind. The Almighty's voice, gentle yet insistent. *They are blinded by fear. It falls to you to guide them.*

Benedict's eyes blazed with otherworldly light. The Elders fell silent, witnessing the change in his demeanour.

"Benedict, what have you become?" Elder Mordant's voice trembled. "This power will consume you, destroy everything!"

But Benedict could feel the dark, intoxicating force surging through him. He embraced it fully, seeking the Almighty's guidance.

There will be those who seek to stand in our way. Do not let them.

"You cling to the past, to traditions that have held us back," Benedict declared. "But I have seen the future, where the Order of Crimson stands tall. I will not rest until that future becomes reality, no matter the cost."

With a wave of his hands, dark tendrils of energy snaked through the air, encircling the Elders. They gasped, struggling against the ethereal bonds.

"I spare your lives only because you may yet serve a purpose," Benedict said quietly. "But make no mistake, the time of the Elders' rule is over. The Order will be reborn, shaped by my hand and guided by the Almighty."

The Elders, pale and stricken, could only nod in submission.

Benedict released his hold, the tendrils dissipating. He strode towards the doors, pausing at the threshold. "Do not defy me or speak against the Almighty's will again, or you will not live to regret it."

With those final words, he stepped out, the doors closing behind him with a resounding thud.

As Benedict descended the winding staircase, a sense of calm and purpose filled him. The Order was on the brink of a new dawn, and he was destined to lead.

In the courtyard, the eyes of the Order were upon him. Novices, acolytes, warriors, and scholars all watched, waiting.

"The path ahead will not be easy," he whispered to the stars above. "But I will not falter. The Order of Crimson will rise again, stronger than ever. And all who stand against us will learn to fear the name of the Crimson Shepherd, chosen of the Almighty."

A sense of purpose swelled within him. The name of the Crimson Shepherd would soon be spoken with reverence and awe.

16
DELIA

Delia picked up another glass and let it sink into the soapy dishwater. She was cleaning up after dinner, the clink of dishes punctuating her thoughts. Despite the simplicity of the task, her mind was wound tight with worry, especially where Kitty was concerned.

Kitty, seated at the kitchen table, watched Delia with an amused expression. “You know, I’m feeling much better. I can cook tomorrow,” she insisted.

Delia shook her head. “Nonsense, you need to rest. Besides, I enjoy doing this. Makes me feel...normal, after all that’s happened.”

“But you’re fussing over me like I’m a child.” Kitty chuckled. “I think you're being a bit over-protective, Delia.”

Delia paused, leaning against the counter, dishcloth in hand. “Maybe I am,” she admitted. “But can you blame me? After these last few weeks, everything I’ve put you through...”

Her voice trailed off, the weight of recent events momentarily clouding her face.

Kitty grinned at her. "It's been the highlight of my year – actually, I haven't had this much excitement in decades! I thought you moving to a small town would be the epitome of boredom, but you've surprised me."

"Rather too much surprise, I'd think," said Delia. "You've been kidnapped by a magical cult and sent unconscious by magic – I was so scared of losing you, and it would all have been my fault."

Kitty sighed. "I don't blame you for any of it, you know. You've been thrown in the deep end here, even more than me. If it wasn't for your magic powers, I'd be feeling sorry for you instead of ragingly envious!"

Delia sighed. "You're a tough nut. I should give you more credit for that. I just can't help but worry."

Kitty leaned forward, her eyes gentle. "Why don't you invite the grandkids back for the weekend? Give yourself someone else to focus on. Or, maybe," she added with a knowing look, "you could go after that handsome cowboy. I'm sure there are plenty more abandoned huts around here..."

Delia gave a mock scowl, tossing the dishcloth onto the counter. "Stop that. Besides, I can't run off with a man and leave my best friend to fend for herself. Aren't I allowed to look after you?"

Kitty reached out, her hand resting atop Delia's. "I appreciate it, I really do. But you also need to take care of yourself. Maybe go for a walk in the woods, visit the market, or have a cuppa with Marjie and the others. You need a break from being my nursemaid."

Delia sighed, a smile slowly returning to her face. "Perhaps a bit of fresh air might do me some good. And the grandkids would certainly liven things up around here."

Kitty nodded, her smile widening. "Exactly. And I promise, I'll start pulling my weight around here. Starting with breakfast tomorrow."

Delia laughed, the sound filling the kitchen with warmth. "Don't you dare, Kitty Hatton. You're to rest and let me pamper you."

As she resumed her cleaning, Delia felt a sense of peace settle over her. The eerie peace of the Clochar still haunted her, as did the fright she'd had over nearly loosing Kitty, but the grounded peace of her cottage and time spent laughing with her best friend had soothed her nerves a little.

"Anything new with that dashingly handsome cowboy?" Kitty asked, her eyes twinkling with curiosity as she watched Delia tidy up the kitchen.

Delia hesitated. She'd been wondering the same thing, herself. "I don't know, really. I haven't seen him since he helped with the rescue the other night."

Kitty nodded thoughtfully. "He really put his all into casting those portals to save you. I should thank him," she said. "Or perhaps you might like to do that yourself, in private."

Delia rebuked her with a playful swat of the tea towel. "Stop that, you. There's no pretending there isn't...or wasn't something. But I just don't know what it is, or if it's all just flamed out. He looked so tired and drained after the portal fiasco."

Kitty shook her head, unsatisfied. "But you were trapped in a cabin with him during a snowstorm. You must have some *details*."

Delia's cheeks flushed a deeper shade of red. "You make it sound like a penny romance novel. Well..."

Kitty let out a cackle. "Oh, stop being coy. Spill."

"You're not getting any details, no matter how much you tease."

Crossing her arms, Kitty said, "Come on, I have to live vicariously through you, remember. I don't have a life here, no magic, no lovers..."

Delia caught the hint of sadness in Kitty's eyes and set the tea towel aside, moving to wrap her friend in a hug. "I'm just glad you're alive, Kitty. Can't that be enough for now?"

Hugging Delia back, Kitty replied softly, "Ditto. When I realised you were missing, I was worried senseless. But you're fussing over me too much now. I'm not made of glass, you know. We need some lively distractions around here. Bring those magical children back."

The corners of Delia's mouth twitched upwards. "Alright, you've convinced me. I'd worry about putting them in harm's way, but I actually feel more relaxed when I can keep an eye on them and protect them. I'll call Gilly tonight."

There was a knock at the door.

Delia opened it to find Ferg, Myrtlewood's mayor, standing on her doorstep. His bright purple robe made him hard to miss, even in the dim evening light.

"Can I help you?" Delia asked, her tone firm. "And before you start, this better not be about the theatre troupe. I have quite enough to be getting on with."

Ferg's expression fell, his usually pompous demeanour giving way to a look of earnest appeal. "It is a great disappointment to hear you say that. The town needs theatre to lift our spirits. It has been a trying time for the troupe in recent months. I must admit, the winter solstice performance wasn't our best, and our players felt they did not live up to their talents in the last show. Your presence at our recent meeting lifted spirits."

Before Delia could respond, Kitty appeared at her side. "Don't listen to her," she interjected, her eyes twinkling with mischief. "Theatre is just what you need, Delia."

Delia gave Kitty a sideways glance, her eyebrow raised. "And since when did you become my life coach?"

Kitty shrugged, a playful smile on her lips. "I've always been your life coach, don't you deny it."

Delia looked back at Ferg, who was watching the exchange with a hopeful look. "I'm not sure now is the right time for me to..."

Ferg interrupted, his voice taking on a persuasive tone. "Delia, your talent, your presence, it would mean so much. And think of the joy it could bring, not just to you, but to the whole town."

Delia sighed, torn between her desire for peace and the desire to be helpful, not to mention the pull of the stage – even the small stage. The last theatre meeting had been a lot of fun, after all. She glanced back at Kitty, whose gave her an encouraging nod.

"Alright, Ferg," Delia finally conceded, "I'll think about dropping by. But I make no promises."

Ferg's face brightened, his usual pomp returning. "Splendid! You won't regret it."

Delia turned to Kitty. "What have you got me into?"

"Don't give me that," Kitty said. "I saw the way you lit up when we went along last time. It really was such fun."

Delia couldn't help but shake her head at Kitty's enthusiasm, yet there was a small spark of excitement within her that she couldn't quite deny.

Sighing, Delia leaned against the doorframe, a hint of a smile tugging at the corners of her mouth. "I suppose a return to normalcy would be nice, and I do need something to keep me occupied."

“This is most excellent!" Ferg said, then he executed an elaborate bow, his purple robe swishing dramatically. "I am at your service, Ms Spark. Let me know if there's anything you need. Anything at all."

"Uhh, thank you..." Delia replied, slightly taken aback by his flourish.

Ferg straightened up, beaming with satisfaction. "The next meeting is the day after tomorrow at two-thirty in the afternoon. Can I count on your attendance?"

Delia glanced over at Kitty, who was rubbing her hands together with a gleeful expression. "This will get you off my back for a bit," Kitty said, barely containing her excitement.

Narrowing her eyes in mock suspicion, Delia replied, "Don't count on it."

As Ferg departed with a final, enthusiastic nod, Delia closed the door and turned to face Kitty. "You sly fox."

Kitty laughed, her eyes sparkling with mischief. "You'll thank me later. You're a natural on the stage, Delia. It's where you belong."

Delia couldn't help but smile, despite her reservations.

Kitty's laughter filled the room, and despite herself, Delia couldn't help but chuckle. Maybe a return to the theatre was exactly what she needed to shake off the shadows of recent events. After all, life was a stage, and perhaps it was time for her to play a more active role once again.

17
Marjie

Marjie strolled casually down the street, bracing herself slightly. She hadn’t seen her good friend Papa Jack for days. The delicate chime of the bell above the door announced her arrival at Myrtlewood Chocolates.

She looked around the shop, taking in the warm, inviting atmosphere, the sage green and lavender colours that always soothed her, and the rich sweet aromas in the air.

"Marjie!" Papa Jack greeted her from behind the counter, his weathered face creasing with a warm smile. "It's so good to see you. I’ve missed you recently."

Marjie approached the counter with a soft smile. "I've missed you too. I thought I'd stop by for a little pick-me-up. Do you have some of your famous hot chocolate for me?"

“I’m just about to brew up a fresh batch.” Papa Jack's eyes twinkled as he reached for a tray of delicate chocolates. "And if you want a pick-me-up, you've come to the right place. Here, try these new truffles I've been working on."

"What flavour?" Marjie asked, though she'd already popped a chocolate into her mouth, savouring the aromatic and rich flavour as it melted on her tongue. Almost instantly, she felt a wave of calm wash over her, the tension in her shoulders easing.

"Lemon balm and bergamot," Papa Jack replied. "To ease the mind and lift the spirits."

"These are splendid," she said, her voice filled with wonder. "You've outdone yourself."

"I'm glad you like them," he replied with a warm smile. "Now, let me see about that drink."

As Papa Jack busied himself with preparing the hot chocolate, he glanced over at her, his expression one of concern.

"How are you holding up, dear?" Marjie asked him. "How's the family settling in?"

He beamed back at her. "Oh, it's been so wonderful having them all back together these past few months. And little Zoya is thriving at school. She's made so many friends. Myrtlewood is really working wonders for us."

"That's lovely to hear," Marjie said as her friend set a steaming mug of hot chocolate in front of her. "I'm so glad they're doing well."

"Speaking of family," Papa Jack continued, his tone shifting to one of concern, "any word from your brother Graham in Yorkshire?"

The mention of her estranged sibling sent a pang through Marjie's heart. She shook her head, her gaze dropping to the countertop. "No, he still won't return my calls. I've left messages, sent letters...but nothing."

"I know it's been hard on you, my dear," Papa Jack said, reaching across the counter to pat her hand. "But maybe it's time for a more...direct approach."

Marjie sighed, the weight of the past settling heavily on her shoulders. "It's just...Graham's always resented my magic, ever since we were children..." She swallowed hard, blinking back the sting of tears. "Magic couldn't save our youngest brother – like I've told you. Graham washed his hands of all of it. It's been years since we've spoken."

Papa Jack nodded with understanding. "Grief can make people do strange things, Marjie. It can twist them up inside, make them lash out at the ones they love most."

"I know," Marjie said, her voice barely above a whisper. "But it still hurts, being shut out like this when I'm making a real effort."

"Sometimes, you've got to stand on someone's doorstep to make them listen," Papa Jack said. "Might be you'll need to pay your brother a visit in person."

Marjie sighed. "Maybe you're right," she conceded, the prospect daunting yet somehow freeing.

The comforting scent of rich hot chocolate and the soft murmur of Papa Jack's voice were anchors in the swirling sea of her thoughts.

"You know, I think I will," Marjie said, resolution settling in her heart. "It's time to mend what's been broken, even if it means stepping out of my comfort zone. I can't let the past dictate my future anymore."

Papa Jack smiled, pride and understanding shining in his eyes. "That's the spirit, Marjie. And remember, you've got the whole town behind you, no matter what happens. We're here for you."

Marjie felt a swell of gratitude, the warmth of Papa Jack's words enveloping her like a comforting embrace. "Thank you. That means more than you know."

There was so much he still didn't know about her, about the Crones. Marjie had been keeping their secrets – she'd sworn not to tell anyone – but now Covvey, Rosemary, and Athena all knew the whole story, as did a handful of others. It seemed only right that she tell her other closest friend, but as she glanced back over the counter at him, his warm smile meeting hers yet again, she decided not to worry him. He had enough on his plate taking care of the family and practically running Rosemary's shop a lot of the time. She would tell him at some point, but not today.

Instead, Marjie savoured her magical hot chocolate, the promise of a new journey lending a hopeful note to the rich, spicy flavour.

18
DECLAN

In the depths of the forest, Declan paused, his hand resting on the glowing seer's stone. Declan eyed the seer’s stone with disdain. He didn't want to respond to the Order, but there were too many risks in ignoring the call.

The image of Father Benedict shimmered into focus, more formidable and desperate than before. Declan felt a knot of anxiety in his stomach, a sensation he still wasn’t properly reacquainted with, after so many centuries.

"Tracker." Father Benedict's voice was icy. "You've broken your sacred oath. Do you realise the peril you've put yourself in?"

Declan clenched his jaw, his eyes hardening. He held the stone up, meeting Benedict's gaze with a defiant expression. "I know what I did," he said calmly. "And I don't regret it. Keep your money. I don't want a penny from you."

Benedict's frown deepened. "You were bound by sacred

oath. You've not only betrayed the contract, but you've also made an enemy of the Order of Crimson."

A smirk played on Declan's lips. "Breaking that contract and defying the Order is my greatest triumph in recent memory."

It was true, though there was far more to the story. In defying the order, and in the magic of his union with Delia, Declan had somehow freed himself from a much older and more powerful bond, but he wasn't about to crow about that to the man who wanted nothing more than total control of every situation he encountered.

Benedict's face twisted into a scowl. "You're playing a dangerous game, Tracker. I know about your proclivity for staying alive, and I have my ways of ensuring that comes to an end."

Declan kept his expression calm despite the chill running down his spine. He hadn't spoken of his immortality to anyone in centuries. How could Benedict possibly know? The revelation caught him off guard, and for a moment, he struggled to maintain his composure.

"I suggest you tread carefully, Benedict," Declan said, his voice steady despite the turmoil inside. "The Order may be a formidable enemy, but I am not afraid of your wrath."

Benedict sneered. "We'll see how far that takes you."

“Will that be all?” Declan asked, keeping his tone neutral, uninterested.

“You may think you’re immortal, tracker,” Benedict continued. “But the Order is a far more powerful enemy than you’ve ever encountered.”

Declan thought back over the centuries of his existence, trying to see if the claim rang true. It was hard to tell when the years and decades all blended together into a seething mass of unresolved pain and torment – sensations he'd been numb to for far too long until his recent awakening. He allowed himself to feel them now, burning up inside like someone who'd stepped too close to a roaring furnace. He deserved this pain – the pain he'd inflicted on others.

"Do not assume," Benedict continued, "that we do not have the power to destroy you. You may have lived a far longer life than most, but all that will come to a swift end unless you fall back in line."

Declan laughed. "Don't tempt me with promises of death that you cannot deliver."

Indeed, death was something he'd longed for over and over, for so long that Declan could not help still revelling in the promise of its release.

Benedict's eyes gleamed. "The Order always delivers, and we know your weakness."

A deeper concern crept into Declan's mind. Either Benedict was bluffing, or he really did have an idea of how to end the immortality that had plagued Declan for so long. Only now, he had a reason for living. He couldn't leave Delia now, not when he'd been granted a new lease on life. Of course, she was his true weakness. The Order could use her to manipulate him – they could go after her family.

A plan began to formulate in his mind. He had to leave.

"Whatever you know," Declan said, "it won't be enough. You'll never catch me."

"We'll see about that," said Father Benedict. "I do believe you'll be seeing us rather soon."

As the image in the stone faded, Declan was left alone in the forest, the weight of Benedict's words pressing down on him. The cool breeze rustled the leaves above, and the earthy scent of the forest filled his nostrils, grounding him in the moment.

Declan's thoughts raced, torn between two opposing desires. Delia had brought a sense of renewed hope and purpose, a light in the darkness that had consumed him for so long. Yet, even as his heart yearned to be with her, Declan knew that his presence only put Delia at further risk. The Order would stop at nothing to punish him for his betrayal. The less connection he had to her, the better.

The Order already sought to punish the Crones, and Delia had been used as a pawn by them in ways that were unforgivable. More than that, the Order sought to steal their power, yet here was evidence that the Crimson Shepherd could be distracted with the urge to stamp out anything that thwarted him in order to maintain his illusions of control. Declan could work with that. He could use Benedict's obsessive nature against him – to distract him from pursuing Delia and her friends.

Unfortunately, staying nearby only increased the danger Delia was in.

With a heavy sigh, Declan extinguished the fire, the embers hissing as they died out. He reconsidered all the possibilities with tactical precision. The best strategic move was not his preferred option, but he had to keep Delia safe, no matter the cost. He would have to leave, to draw the Order's attention away from Myrtlewood and onto himself. Delia might not like it; then again, he had no idea what she thought of him now. Was their time together a mere dalliance for her, or something more? Either way, leaving town was a sacrifice he was willing to make, even if it meant losing the one person who had made him feel alive again.

19
DELIA

Delia was surprised to find herself feeling excited as she approached the town hall, ready to help out with another meeting of the Myrtlewood Players. She still hadn't learnt anyone's names, aside from Ferg. At the first meeting she'd attended, she'd felt nervous to start off with and she'd felt she'd somewhat been dragged into being there, but this time was different. She looked around at the group, to see some of the same faces from last time, as well as some new additions.

Ferg sat regally, wearing a bright violet cloak. Sherry from the pub perched on the seat next to him, and beside her were two teenagers. Delia smiled encouragingly, hoping to instil some confidence in the young newcomers. The first introduced herself as Ashwagandha, "Ash for short," and she was a bright young woman of Indian heritage.

Next to Ash, the other teenager spoke up. "Uhh, hi...I'm Sam, and my pronouns are they/them. If that's okay..." Sam said, nervously. "I mean. I've heard people from outside the magical world can get angry about people not fittin into the labels they're used to..."

"That's more than okay," said Delia. "I'm used to the West End where no one cares about fitting in – unless it's fitting into a specific role, of course. I'm glad you're here, Sam."

Sam looked flushed, but their eyes shone brightly. "I'm...I suppose I'm quite shy, but I really want to help out..."

"We were excited to hear that a real director had joined up," Ash added.

Ferg cleared his throat. "Excuse me? I am a renowned director! I just have other things on my plate right now, being mayor and so on." He looked down at his fingernails as if suddenly finding them fascinating.

Delia turned her attention to the rest of the group to complete the introductions. A tall black woman, Sid, told Delia she was also head of the local fire department. "Rumour has it you've had a few issues with fire yourself."

Delia chuckled. "Yes, it's probably a good thing that we've met. I'll be sure to stay in your good books in case I have any more misfires with my powers, so to speak."

An older man, Frederic Aventurine, introduced himself next. It turned out he taught at the local school, in a subject that sounded so mysterious that Delia forgot it at once. Next to him, sat two women, the first called Tamsyn, with greying dark blonde hair, and another called Nesta, with darker hair, a kind face, and a gentle Welsh lilt to her accent. As the others continued to introduce themselves, Delia lost track of all the names.

Delia clapped her hands, the sound echoing through the bustling room. "Let's get started with some warm-up exercises. Find a partner and stand facing each other."

As the group paired off, Delia found herself standing opposite Sid, the tall, athletic firefighter. Sid grinned at her, eyes sparkling with anticipation. Delia couldn't help but return the smile, feeling the infectious energy of the room.

"We'll begin with 'Mirrors'," Delia explained. "One person will lead, making slow, deliberate movements, while the other mirrors them as accurately as possible. Remember, the goal is to move in sync with your partner."

Delia raised her right hand slowly, and Sid followed suit with her left. They began to move through a series of gestures, their pace measured and steady. Around them, laughter erupted as pairs fumbled through the exercise.

As the exercise continued, Delia let her gaze wander around the room. Ash and Sam, the young newcomers, moved with an almost eerie synchronicity. Tamsyn and Nesta, despite their contrasting personalities, found a playful harmony in their mirrored movements.

After a few minutes, Delia called out, "Great work, everyone! Now, let's switch roles and try again."

This time, Delia paired with Frederic, the eccentric school teacher. Despite his initial awkwardness, Frederic soon found his rhythm, his movements growing more fluid and confident.

After a few more rounds, Delia called for a break. As the group dispersed, chattering excitedly, she took a moment to centre herself. She felt at home here – the energy in the room was electric, a buzz that left her skin tingling. This, she realised, was what she had been missing – the thrill of creative collaboration and the chemistry of performance.

Rejuvenated, Delia gathered the group once more. "Now, let's move on to a new game – 'Character Walks'. Choose a character to embody, exploring how they move, hold themselves, and interact with the world around them."

As the Myrtlewood Players began to transform, Delia watched with a broad smile. Sherry glided across the room with the poise of a grand dame, while Ash's steps were light and mischievous, a pixie in human form. Sam's movements were careful and deliberate, a contrast to Sid's confident, no-nonsense stride.

Delia called out different scenarios – a royal ball, a haunted forest, a bustling market – and the group responded, their characters adapting and evolving. The room came alive with imagined interactions.

As the exercises came to a close, Delia's heart swelled with a feeling she had sorely missed since her former career had gone up in flames: pride. This odd bunch of individuals, each bringing their own unique talents and perspectives, had the potential to create something wonderful.

“Alright!” Delia called out, drawing everyone's attention. “Let's settle down and discuss your plans. What’s on the horizon for the Myrtlewood Players? I’m not sure how long I’m sticking around for,” she said, and a sad murmur sounded around the group. “But, hey, it's a new year, and I'm curious to hear what you all have in mind."

Ferg raised his hand. "I propose we do A Midsummer Night's Dream again. It's a classic and always a crowd-pleaser."

Groans echoed around the room. Sherry spoke up. "We've done that play so many times. Can't we try something new?"

Sid nodded in agreement. "Ferg, we've done Shakespeare to death. Let's put A Midsummer Night’s Dream into a long winter hibernation and do something fresh.”

Ferg leaned forward, his brow furrowed. "What do you suggest, then? It's not easy to find something that will please everyone.”

Before anyone could respond, Sam timidly raised their hand. "Um, I know we’re new to the group but Ash has written a script. It's really good, and maybe we could consider it for one of our productions?"

Delia noticed a few sceptical looks being exchanged around the room.

Ash, who had been sitting quietly, straightened up. "Yes, I've written a play. It's a bit different from what the Myrtlewood Players usually do...”

“But I think it could be really engaging,” said Sam encouragingly.

Ferg's eyebrows shot up. "A newcomer writing our script? That's not how we usually do things."

Sherry chimed in, "But it could be just the shake-up we need. The concept sounds intriguing, Ash."

Frederic looked intrigued but cautious. "What's it about?"

Ash took a deep breath. "It's a story of mythic transformation. My play is called 'Cailleach and Brìghde – The Cycle of Death and Rebirth.' Uhh, that's a working title so please help me come up with a better name."

"It sounds fascinating," said Delia. "Tell us more."

Ash took a deep breath and continued. "Okay...It's based on the myth of the Cailleach, the ancient goddess of winter, and Brìghde, who is...you know, one of the names for Brigid, the goddess of spring. The story explores their cyclical struggle and eventual balance, reflecting the themes of death and rebirth."

The room fell silent as Ash continued, gaining confidence with each word. "On an internal level, the imprisonment and release of Brigid represents an individual's journey through psychological winter, like depression or stagnation, to the renewal and growth of spring. It's about personal transformation and development, the cycles we all go through in life."

Delia was impressed. This was far more profound than she had expected. "Ash, this sounds like a powerful and relevant story. I think it has the potential to connect with our audience on a deep level."

Nesta added, "It's certainly timely. Our community has been through a lot, and a story of renewal and resilience could be very meaningful."

Ferg, who had been uncharacteristically quiet, finally spoke up. "Are the Myrtlewood Players ready to take on something so different and contemporary? We have a lot of new members this year."

Tamsyn interjected, "I think it's great that Ash has taken

the initiative to write something original. It might be just the fresh start we need."

Delia sensed the tension and decided to step in. "Why don't we take a democratic approach? All those in favour of reading Ash's script and considering it for our next production, raise your hand."

Slowly, hands began to rise. Sam's shot up first, followed by Sherry, Sid, Nesta, and Tamsyn. Ferg was the last to agree, looking a bit perturbed.

Delia grinned. "Then it's settled. Ash, please send around copies of your script. We'll read it over the week and reconvene next time to discuss it further."

She caught Ferg's eye as everyone prepared to leave. He gave her a tight smile, clearly still processing this unexpected turn of events.

Kitty was smiling smugly from the back of the room, having slipped in halfway through. She gave Delia two thumbs up as the meeting drew to a close.

Delia joined Kitty and they slipped on their coats and stepped out into the crisp evening air. Delia took a deep breath, the chill invigorating her senses. She turned to Kitty with a surprised smile. "You know, I rather enjoyed myself tonight," she admitted.

Kitty, wrapping her scarf tighter around her neck, gave Delia a knowing look. "You sounded quite invested, especially in that new play."

Delia nodded, her breath misting before her. "I'll have to read it first, but Ash certainly seems to be a bright spark."

Kitty beamed, her eyes reflecting the soft glow of the street-lights. "I told you this was exactly what you needed."

As they reached the end of the street, Delia glanced back at the town hall, its windows darkening as the last of the Players left. This small town might not have the prestige of the West End, but it had far more heart than ego, and perhaps that was the greater reward.

20

INGRID

Ingrid's boots squelched as she made her way determinedly through the dense swamp, the earth dragon in her puppy form bounding alongside her, paws sinking into the soft, muddy ground with each enthusiastic leap. The mist swirled around them, a veil of moisture that clung to Ingrid's cloak and the dragon puppy's fur, creating a shimmering halo in the diffused light.

As they ventured deeper, a jagged outline loomed ahead, emerging from the haze like a ghostly apparition. Ingrid's heart quickened, her mind veering back to that fateful night in the swamp – the winter solstice when the earth dragon had first burst forth from her ancient prison.

The now-broken keystone, once a towering monolith, lay partially submerged in the murky waters, its once solid presence reduced to a jumble of moss-covered rocks and rubble.

Yet, as Ingrid approached, a flicker of hope ignited within her. Perhaps, hidden among the debris, lay the object of her quest.

"Look, it's the keystone where you first emerged!" Ingrid called out to the dragon puppy, who was momentarily distracted by a dragonfly darting erratically above the water's surface. The dragon puppy's tail wagged furiously as she leapt and bounded, trying to catch the elusive insect, her paws sending ripples across the stagnant water.

Ingrid couldn't help but smile at the dragon puppy's antics, even as a sense of urgency tugged at her thoughts. The energy in the swamp churned and pulsed, as if trying to convey a message, adding to the nagging stream of ideas that had refused to leave her in peace since their visit to the Elders Blaze Grove.

That encounter on the cloud island had changed something deep within Ingrid, sparking a sensation she hadn't experienced in years: jealousy. Agatha, with her quick wit and sharp tongue, had managed to secure a sacred relic – a dragon stone that pulsed with the power of the air element. Ingrid had read about such artifacts in ancient tomes, but had never paid them much heed until she'd seen the sparkling crystal resting in Agatha's palm.

Sure, Ingrid had the earth dragon herself, a creature of immense power and wisdom, but why was there no stone, no tangible relic to help her connect and communicate with this ancient and playful beast?

Ingrid paused by the keystone rubble, her gaze scanning the muddy ground tangled with roots and vines. The dragon puppy, her brown coat tinged with a green sheen that perfectly camouflaged her in the swamp's verdant hues, splashed into a nearby pool, sending murky water flying as she pounced on a floating leaf.

"Careful there, oh wise one!" Ingrid laughed, watching the dragon puppy's antics. "We've got a relic to find, remember?"

The dragon puppy, seemingly unbothered by Ingrid's gentle admonishment, continued her playful exploration of the swamp, her nose twitching as she sniffed at the damp earth and tangled roots.

Ingrid's mind drifted back to the ancient grimoire she had consulted after their journey from the grove to the sky island. The words that had materialised before her eyes had filled her with a burning determination, now echoing in her mind and compelling her to continue the search: "For each element, a sacred stone, a relic of power."

Agatha had had no trouble in locating her relic, the air dragon's pendant. But where was the earth stone? Ingrid refused to dismiss the passage as mere metaphor, a poetic illustration of the balance of forces. Not now that Agatha's pendant had proven to be real and tangible, a physical manifestation of the air element and the dragon itself.

Ingrid was acutely aware that her envy of Agatha's stone was somewhat juvenile, a petty emotion unbefitting a woman of her age and wisdom. Yet, it had been so long since she'd experienced the hot, tight twinge of jealousy that it gave her pause, forcing her to pay closer attention to the feelings stirring within her.

Long ago, Ingrid had learned to trust her emotions – not always in how they first appeared, but in the deeper messages they conveyed. If the air dragon had a relic, then surely there must be one for the earth element as well.

The earth dragon had first appeared here, emerging from the very keystone that now lay in ruins. Ingrid wondered how long the creature had lain dormant, hidden away in hibernation, waiting for the right moment to awaken.

Ingrid's irritation at the ancient being's choice to take on the form of a playful, juvenile creature had initially puzzled her. But now, as she watched the dragon puppy splash and play, she began to suspect that this form was a test of sorts, a challenge to look beyond appearances and uncover the true nature of the beast.

"Remember, the air dragon has a pendant," Ingrid mused aloud, drawing the attention of the dragon puppy, who tilted her head quizzically. "And the book says there are other relics too. Come on, girl. We've got to find the sacred earth stone! Where could it be? You must know."

Ingrid crouched down, her fingers tracing the mossy surface of one of the boulders that had once been part of the keystone. The dragon puppy trotted over, nuzzling Ingrid's hand with her wet snout, her warm breath tickling Ingrid's skin.

"What do you think, little pebble?" Ingrid asked, gently tapping the dragon puppy's nose.

The dragon puppy glared at her, clearly unimpressed with the nickname. But Ingrid held her ground, a smile tugging at the corners of her mouth.

"I'm going to call you Pebble if you insist on staying in this tiny, juvenile form," Ingrid declared. "Sure, it's convenient when we have visitors, but..."

Ingrid's words trailed off as she glanced around the swamp, a sudden thought striking her. If the Order or the Sisterhood were watching, the dragon's current form would be an excellent way to avoid drawing attention. And, if they were to come under attack, the puppy's unassuming appearance would give them a significant advantage, allowing them to catch their enemies off guard.

With a grin, Ingrid gave the dragon puppy a scratch behind the ears, silently commending her for her cleverness. Then, with a determined nod, she returned to the task at hand.

"Come on, Pebble. Is the relic hidden here, buried somewhere in the swamp? Or does it need a special condition to reveal itself?"

The earth dragon yipped excitedly and spun in a circle, her tail wagging so vigorously that her entire body shook. It was as if she was trying to communicate something, a message that Ingrid couldn't quite decipher.

Ingrid laughed, standing up and surveying the murky waters that stretched out before them. "You're right, the answer is out there somewhere. This swamp keeps its secrets well, doesn't it?"

With a determined nod, Ingrid stepped away from the keystone rubble, the dragon puppy bounding ahead of her, splashing through the shallow pools and leaving a trail of ripples in her wake. "Alright, my infuriatingly playful friend, let's see what other clues we can find."

The water that pooled around her feet was dark and still,

like a mirror reflecting the twisted shapes of the gnarled trees and hanging moss. In these reflections, Ingrid saw not just the swamp, but glimpses of deeper truths, the interconnectedness of all things.

The dragon puppy, who had been chasing a frog, paused and looked up at Ingrid, her eyes gleaming with a wisdom that belied her youthful form.

"You sense it too, don't you?" Ingrid asked, meeting the dragon puppy's gaze. "The swamp is trying to teach us something, about patience, about resilience. The relic will reveal itself when the time is right."

The dragon puppy yipped in agreement and dashed off into the underbrush, her tail held high. Ingrid followed, pushing through the dense foliage. "What secrets do you hold, little Pebble?" Ingrid called out.

The dragon paused, glancing back at Ingrid with a mischievous glint in her eye. It was as if she knew exactly what Ingrid was seeking, but was choosing to keep the knowledge hidden.

"Hah! Keeping your secrets then, are you?" Ingrid laughed, shaking her head in amusement and frustration. Then, with a sigh, she added, "I suppose I'll just have to keep looking."

21
DECLAN

Declan's boots crunched on the frosty gravel as he approached the front door of Delia's cottage. His breath formed clouds in the frigid air, the scent of impending snow mingling with the evening's sharp chill.

He hesitated for a moment, his hand hovering over the door knocker. Giving Delia space had seemed right, after all she and Kitty had been through, but now? The need to see her, to ensure she was alright before he left town gnawed at him.

Declan stood before the quaint facade of the cottage for a moment longer as the last wisps of daylight cast long shadows across the garden path.

He hesitated, his hand hovering just inches from the door. It had been some time since he'd last seen her, since the chaos of the portal and the uncertainty that followed.

He had told her she could call on him any time, yet she

hadn't, so he'd given her time out of respect, but to leave without telling her in person seemed a greater disrespect.

The chill in the air bit at his skin. The scent of more impending snow hung in the air, along with the scent of woodsmoke from the chimneys of Myrtlewood, filling the evening with a crispness that spoke of change, of cycles ending and beginning anew.

He knew that leaving Delia now seemed to be one of the hardest things he'd had to do, though he couldn't quite understand why. Some feelings, after all, were beyond comprehension.

He wished he could take her with him, though she had her own life to be getting on with. Besides, certain journeys had to be made alone, and this was one of them.

But he couldn't leave without telling her. His heart felt like a stone in his chest, heavy with the weight of unspoken truths and roads yet to be travelled.

He shoved his hands into his pockets, seeking warmth, seeking solace.

There was so much Delia didn't know about him. If she caught even a glimpse of the full extent of his past, the violence of war and quieter battles, would she look at him with the same warmth? Or would that warmth be replaced by a coldness to match the approaching winter's night?

Regret clawed at him. He had always been solitary when he'd had the choice, but Delia...Delia had managed to pierce through his solitude, to make him wish for things he'd long since given up hope for.

For now, he had to disappear into the shadows once more.

With a steadying breath, Declan rapped his knuckles against the door, the sound cutting through his own resistance.

He needed to see her, even if his presence, or the words he carried, might be unwelcome. The wait, marked by the rhythm of his heartbeat in his ears, stretched out. How could it be that he'd lived for so many centuries and yet time could still pass far too slowly in a moment like this?

The door swung open, and Delia's face broke into a warm, surprised smile, breaking through his own resistance.

"Declan," she said, her voice filled with subtle joy. "What brings you here?"

Kitty's head popped around the corner, her eyes gleaming with mirth. "Well, if it isn't our hero," she teased. "Come to sweep Delia off her feet?"

"Come in," Delia said, stepping aside. "It's cold out there."

22

DELIA

Moments earlier, Delia had been helping Kitty get ready to go out as she'd been invited for dinner at Una and Ashwyn's. Delia wasn't in the mood to leave the house, but she wished her friend well and told her to stay out of trouble.

Kitty rolled her eyes. "Darling, I am trouble! You know that."

"Well, keep it to a minimum," said Delia.

"And what about you? No wild parties while I'm out," Kitty teased, adjusting her scarf in the mirror.

Delia laughed, playfully rolling her eyes. "I think I can manage to restrain myself for one evening."

There was a sudden knock at the door, a sound that seemed unusually loud in the peaceful setting of the cottage. Delia gave Kitty a curious look before heading to answer it.

Declan was at the door and Delia didn't know what to do.

He hesitated when she invited him in, a grave look in his eyes. He stepped in, slowly.

Kitty, sensing the change in atmosphere, grabbed her purse. "I'll take this as my cue to leave," she said, giving Delia a meaningful look. "I'll be back late. Don't wait up."

Once Kitty had left, Delia turned back to Declan, concern etching her features. "What's wrong? Are you still not recovered from the rescue?"

Declan shook his head, his gaze still fixed on the ground. "I'm here to let you know that I must leave," he said, his voice low.

"Leave?" Delia echoed, a sense of alarm rising within her.

"I'm going away for a while," Declan continued, finally meeting her gaze. "It's for the best."

Delia felt a rush of emotions – confusion, concern, and a pang of sadness. "But why? What's happened?"

Declan hesitated, as if weighing his words. "It's complicated. I...I need to draw attention away from Myrtlewood. It's the only way to keep you safe."

Delia's heart sank. She understood the gravity of his words, and though she could think of reasons to argue, his mind was clearly already made up. Besides, what hold did she really have over this man? She hardly knew him. Yet, thc thought of him leaving filled her with dread.

"Declan, I..." she started, but words failed her.

Declan stepped forward, placing a gentle hand on her shoulder. "I have to do this, Delia. Please understand. It's the only way."

Delia nodded, her eyes glistening with unshed tears. "I understand. Just...just be careful, okay?"

Declan gave her a small, reassuring smile. "I will. And I'll come back. I promise."

"When are you leaving?" she asked, her voice barely above a whisper.

"At first light," Declan replied, his voice steady but his eyes still avoiding hers.

Why did he always speak in such an old-fashioned way? Delia wondered. He couldn't be a vampire, could he? She'd seen him out in the sun too much for that. She took a deep breath, mustering her courage. "So, you can stay tonight, then?" she asked, a hint of hope in her voice.

At her words, something shifted in Declan. He looked up, and for the first time since he arrived, a spark lit up in his eyes.

Delia allowed a playful smile to touch her lips. "I have wine," she said, trying to lighten the mood. "And it's far more comfortable here than in that abandoned cabin."

Declan's response was a slow nod, accompanied by the faintest hint of a smile. "Yes, I can stay tonight."

Delia smiled as she led him to the warmly lit living room. "Let me get that wine."

They sat together on the sofa, clinking their glasses in celebration of nothing more than the evening they'd chosen to share.

Delia placed her wine glass on the coffee table, her fingers lingering on the stem a moment. She could feel Declan's gaze on her, intense yet uncertain, as if he were wrestling with a storm of thoughts just beneath the surface.

Turning to face him, she found him closer than she had anticipated, their knees almost touching. The air between them fizzled.

Declan cleared his throat. "This wine...it's good."

Delia couldn't help but smile at his attempt to keep the conversation light. "I'm glad you like it."

There was a pause, a fleeting moment where both seemed to hold their breath, caught in the gravity of their proximity. Delia's heart pounded, nervous fluttering in her stomach. She barely knew this man, and yet she *knew* him, not just in the biblical sense, but deeply, emotionally, intuitively.

Slowly, as if drawn by a force neither of them could resist, Declan leaned in closer. Delia found herself closing the distance between them until she could feel the warmth of his skin.

Their eyes locked, Declan's hand reached up, hesitantly, as if he were afraid to break the spell between them. His fingers brushed a strand of hair from her face, a touch so light it sent a shiver through her.

Delia's breath hitched, her eyes fluttering closed for a split second. When she opened them again, Declan was even closer, his face mere inches from hers. She could count the flecks of gold in his eyes, see the faintest crease in his brow.

Time seemed to stand still, the world outside fading away until there was nothing but the two of them, caught in a bubble of tension and desire. Her lips parted slightly, a silent invitation, a question that could be answered only by a kiss.

23
GWYNETH

Gwyneth's steps echoed softly down the herb garden pathway in the pre-dawn stillness as she made her way to the temple. The sky was still a deep indigo, stars fading as the first hint of morning began to gild the horizon. She found sisters Breag and Franwen already inside, illuminated by candlelight.

Gwyneth couldn't help but feel a pang of isolation as she approached them. Despite the Sisterhood's dogma of no hierarchy, Sister Breag held the power here, always insisting that it was the will of the great goddess that guided them. And with Franwen as her devoted acolyte, it was two against one. Gwyneth often longed for the old days when her mentor, Verna, had led the Veiled Sisterhood with grace and empathy, but since her passing Breag had taken over with an entirely different style of leadership.

"Good morning, sisters," Gwyneth said, her voice low and tinged with worry.

“Thank you for taking the time out of your busy morning schedule to join us,” Sister Franwen said.

Gwyneth shot her a quelling look. “I must admit, I deliberated before leaving my chamber. Something is not right with the energy here. We need to talk about Mathilda."

Sister Breag turned to face her, her expression serene yet firm. "Gwyneth, we've been through this. The initiation of the crystal has brought peace to the Clochar. Its potential for the world at large is immense."

Franwen nodded in agreement. "Just think of the harmony it could bring, the balance to the chaos of the outside world."

Gwyneth clasped her hands before her in concern. "But at what cost? I've seen how some of our sisters, those with a lower natural affinity for magic, have been affected. They are waning in energy – never mind that the whole initiative is powered by one of us who is unknowingly sacrificing herself – her lifeforce and magic – all for a bit of peace and quiet.”

“Mathilda happily submits herself for the greater good. You know that. Besides, the sisters with less magic are fine,” Franwen argued.

Gwyneth looked to Sister Breag who merely gazed into the flame of a candle.

“It’s not right,” Gwyneth said. “Some of our sisters are bedridden. There's a...disconnection. If the crystal can do this to them, what might it do to the world at large?"

Breag's gaze hardened slightly. "Change is often accompanied by discomfort, Gwyneth. It's a small price for the greater good."

Gwyneth shook her head, her frustration growing. "It's more than discomfort, Sister Breag. It's a fundamental change in their being; I only hope it's temporary. We still have a chance. We can't ignore the signs now. If we're to believe in balance, we must consider all aspects, not just the benefits."

Franwen's shoulders stiffened. "Gwyneth has a point. If the crystal can alter the essence of our sisters, its effect on those without magical defences could be unpredictable, not to mention the protections on the Clochar."

Breag crossed her arms, her brow furrowed in thought. "Then we must study it further. But we cannot abandon the path we've set upon. The crystal's potential is too great."

Gwyneth felt both relief and apprehension at Breag's concession. "Then, please let us proceed with caution," she urged. "We must understand all the ramifications before we even think of extending its influence beyond the Clochar."

Breag's expression was resolute as she countered Gwyneth's concerns. "We will be fine, Gwyneth. We will do our research and work to avoid problems where we can, but you must understand that some sacrifices are necessary for the greater good. We can't lose sight of our goals for a few unfortunate side effects. The path we've set upon is for the greater good. The great goddess has shown us the way."

Gwyneth's thoughts wandered to Ingrid. "The Crones know about the crystal. They're attuned to magic in ways we can't ignore. And if they sense what we're doing, they'll certainly try to stop it."

Franwen's lips curled in disdain. "That traitor, Ingrid," she muttered. "She's always been too close to the outside world, too involved with those who don't understand our ways."

Breag's eyes sparkled with a calculating gleam. "Ingrid will get what she deserves," she said, a hint of satisfaction in her voice. "She walked right into my trap."

Gwyneth's heart skipped a beat. "Your trap? Why wasn't I informed?"

Breag turned to her, her gaze piercing. "You have a soft spot for Ingrid, Gwyneth. I can tell. It's best you weren't involved."

Gwyneth's voice wavered slightly as she addressed Breag's insinuations. "Do you question my commitment to the sisterhood?" she asked, her eyes searching for some semblance of trust in her fellow elders.

Breag responded, her tone measured yet unyielding. "Not your commitment, perhaps. But we do wonder if there are... other loyalties at play."

Franwen interjected, a sharp edge to her words. "We know you were lovers," she said bluntly. "The scrying bowl showed us."

Gwyneth felt as if the floor had dropped beneath her. The blood drained from her face, leaving her feeling exposed and vulnerable. "That was a long time ago," she managed to say, her voice barely above a whisper. "And you must know, I chose the sisterhood."

"Which is why you're still here," Breag said, her words slow and deliberate. "Though you may never have become an elder if we'd thought to check on that little situation earlier."

The accusation hung heavy in the air, a tangible weight on

Gwyneth's shoulders. She had always worried that her past with Ingrid, though long buried, might one day resurface, but she hadn't expected it to be wielded like a weapon against her, not now after all these years.

Her commitment to the sisterhood had been her guiding light, her unwavering path. Yet now, it seemed, the past she had thought securely locked away was threatening to unravel the very fabric of her present.

Gwyneth straightened her back, her resolve hardening. "My past with Ingrid has no bearing on my dedication to our cause," she stated firmly. "I have always, and will always, put the sisterhood first."

Breag and Franwen exchanged a look, a silent communication that left Gwyneth feeling further isolated. The bonds she thought unbreakable were fraying, and Gwyneth knew that the path ahead would be one of vigilance and, perhaps, solitary defiance. For the good of the sisterhood, and for the integrity of her own soul, she would stand her ground.

Moments later, Gwyneth walked alongside Franwen, the cool air of the early morning brushing against their faces as they left the temple. Her mind was tense with thoughts and emotions, a storm that seemed at odds with the peaceful dawn.

Turning to Franwen, she voiced the doubt that had been gnawing at her. "Don't you ever wonder about all of this?" she asked, her voice barely above a whisper.

Franwen glanced at her, her expression resolute, almost stoic. "We follow a higher power, the will of the great goddess," she said firmly. "Who are we to question?"

Gwyneth's heart sank at the response, the gap in understanding between them widening like a chasm. She yearned for a sign of solidarity, a shared moment of doubt that would make her feel less alone in her concerns.

“Surely, the goddess is great enough to withstand any questioning. Surely, to question is only natural, and the goddess loves all of nature.”

“Perhaps, but you walk a dangerous line now, Gwyneth.” Franwen's next words came as a quiet warning, her gaze fixed on the path ahead. "And I’d keep any questions you have silent, if I were you. Breag is not in the mood to be lenient."

The words struck Gwyneth with the coldness of a winter breeze. She realised the precariousness of her position within the sisterhood. Her past with Ingrid, her rising doubts, they all made her vulnerable in a way she hadn't anticipated.

As they parted ways, Gwyneth's mind raced with the implications of what had transpired. The sisterhood she had devoted her life to, the cause she had believed in so fervently, was it as good and pure as she’d always believed? Was there room for questioning, for growth, within these ancient walls?

24
AGATHA

Agatha trudged up the hill behind her farmhouse, her boots sinking into the soft earth with each determined step. The hill overlooked the vast expanse of her property, a patchwork of fields and forests stretching out under the open sky. In her hand, she clutched the amulet, its surface etched with ancient symbols that whispered of air and flight which she'd carefully studied down to the last detail.

It was time for action.

Reaching the summit, Agatha paused to catch her breath, her gaze sweeping across the landscape. She then focused on the amulet, holding it up before her. "Alright, you," she addressed the inanimate object. "It's time you and I had a little chat."

The amulet remained silent and inert in her palm, its secrets locked away. Agatha frowned, her patience wearing thin. "I know you're connected to the air dragon. It's time to wake up and do...whatever it is you're supposed to do."

The amulet offered no response, its surface dull under the overcast sky. Agatha sighed in frustration. "Come on. I need your help. There are things happening, things I don't fully understand. And you're supposed to be a part of this."

She waited, half-hoping the amulet would spring to life without more effort. But the hilltop remained silent, the only sound the whistling of the breeze.

Agatha's frustration bubbled over as she continued her one-sided argument. "I don't have time for this. If you're going to be any use, you need to start now."

She gazed at the amulet, her brow furrowed, expecting... something, anything. But the amulet remained stubbornly silent, its secrets locked away. Agatha let out a sigh, her shoulders slumping in resignation. "Fine, have it your way," she said, her voice softening.

As she released her tight grip on the amulet, something shifted in the air around her. The breeze picked up, swirling around her in a gentle caress that hummed with magic. Agatha's eyes widened as she felt a presence, a vast and ancient energy that was both exhilarating and intimidating.

Before her, emerging from the pendant in her outstretched hand, the air began to shimmer and coalesce into a spectral figure, a being of pure, swirling wind. The air dragon, majestic and ethereal, appeared before her eyes, its form hazy and transparent, but still impressive.

Agatha stood in awe, her earlier frustration forgotten. The

air dragon rose and moved around her, its essence intertwining with the breeze in a dance of wind and light.

Then, in a voice like a dry whisper, the dragon said, "The winds of change are upon you, Agatha. Embrace them, for they bring growth and renewal."

Agatha listened, her heart racing with excitement and a touch of fear. The air dragon's words were cryptic, yet they resonated deep within her. She knew she was on the cusp of something monumental.

“What is it?” Agatha asked, but it was too late. The dragon's form began to fade, merging back into the pendant. She tried again, several times, to get any other reaction, but nothing happened. The air dragon was back to being elusive and was clearly as stubborn as she was.

Agatha sighed. “Another cryptic warning of change,” she huffed. "There must be a lesson for me here, but I wish it would make itself clear. I suppose I’d better tell the other crones...and Covvey," she whispered to herself.

They needed to know, to understand something big was happening, even if it was infuriatingly vague.

25
THE CLERIC

The Cleric kept his head down. His menial duties hastily completed, blending seamlessly among the other members. They bustled about their daily routines, oblivious to the tempest brewing beneath the Cleric's calm exterior as the sun shone over the compound's neatly kept gardens.

As the Cleric moved through the grounds, the warmth of the early morning sun caressed his face. The light glinted from the ancient stones. The air was fresh, filled with the scent of dew-kissed grass and the distant fragrance of blooming flowers from the citrus orchards. Birds chirped merrily, their melodies a rare form of music in the otherwise sombre atmosphere. For a fleeting moment, the beauty of the day threatened to pierce the veil of the Cleric's dark intentions.

He looked around at the other members of the Order of Crimson in their matching robes and pious expressions.

To them, he was just another penitent soul, atoning for his

transgressions, nothing more than a background figure in the tightly woven fabric of their sacred order.

But today was different. Today, the Cleric was not just another ant in the nest. As the others immersed themselves in their tasks, he slipped away unnoticed, moving with a fresh purpose and energy that had been growing in the days following his fall from grace.

His steps, once hesitant and burdened by doubt, were now decisive, fuelled by a newfound resolve. The Cleric had a plan, a dangerous and audacious scheme that had been taking shape in the darkest corners of his mind.

Everything must end...

He made his way to a secluded corner of the compound, where the shadows were deep and the likelihood of being seen was minimal.

The Cleric's fingers brushed against the cool stone as he walked, tracing the intricate carvings that adorned the walls. These ancient symbols and scripts, once so meaningful, now seemed like cryptic messages from a forgotten time. The dim light created shadows that played across the carvings, giving them a life of their own, a silent language that spoke of secrets and hidden truths. The touch of the stone was a tactile reminder of the history of the Order, a history he was now set to unravel.

There, hidden beneath an old, gnarled tree, he had carefully concealed his charms, constructed in the dead of night with ingredients pilfered from the supply closets he used to manage, the tools of his impending rebellion. These were not the sacred relics of the Order, but rather instruments of an even more devious nature, forged in secrecy and imbued with powers that the Cleric had only ever theorised about and had never dared to wield until now.

With deft fingers, he retrieved the charms from their hiding place, each one humming with magic.

As he passed by the common areas, the muted sounds of the other members going about their duties reached his ears. The clink of dishes being washed, the low murmur of morning prayers, the subtle rustle of robes against the floor – all these familiar sounds now felt distant, as if he were hearing them through a thick veil. The mundane routine of the compound, once a source of comfort and structure, now felt like a noose tightening around his neck, a constant reminder of the life he was about to leave behind.

He proceeded around the compound with a solemn and critical expression, as if checking various pieces of work had been completed. Keeping his head down, he laid out his traps with meticulous care, ensuring that they were well-hidden and would go unnoticed until it was too late.

The Cleric knew the layout of the compound like the back of his hand, and he used this knowledge to his advantage, placing each charm where it would cause the most chaos and destruction.

Once his task was complete, the Cleric took a moment to survey his handiwork. He felt a surge of satisfaction, mixed with a pang of remorse. This was not the path he had envisioned for himself when he first joined the Order, but circumstances had forced his hand. The betrayal he had witnessed, the lies he had been fed, had left him with no other choice.

The Cleric paused for a moment, allowing himself to take in the scene. It was a picture of harmony and devotion, a well-orchestrated dance of piety and service. Yet, beneath the serene surface, he knew there lay a web of lies and deceit. This realisation filled him with a bitter sense of irony. Here, in this place of supposed sanctity, he was about to commit an act of profound treachery. But in his heart, he knew it was a necessary evil, a step towards exposing the truth and tearing down the false idol the Order worshipped as if it were the almighty power of a true god.

As he pondered his next steps, the Cleric's thoughts turned to the wider world. It was not enough to simply destroy the Order of Crimson; he had to go further. The Veiled Sisterhood, the Elemental Crones of Myrtlewood, they too were part of the intricate web of deception that had ensnared him for so long. They all had to be eradicated, swept away in a tide of retribution and cleansing fire.

The Cleric's steps were light as continued on his path. He was no longer a man weighed down by doubt and despair, but rather a force of power, unstoppable and resolute.

The world as he knew it was about to change, and he was the catalyst for that change.

As he disappeared into the nearby forest, the Cleric allowed himself a small smile. The stage was set, the pieces were in motion, and soon, the Order of Crimson, along with everything else he had come to despise, would be nothing but ashes and memories.

As the Cleric stepped out of the confines of the Order's compound, a sense of unaccustomed freedom washed over him. It was a feeling so rare, so exhilarating, that it brought a newfound lightness to his step. For years, his life had been bound by the rigid structure and solemn duties of the Order, each day following the last with unerring precision and discipline.

As he walked along the mountain path, the Cleric's mind wandered back to his youth, to those rare moments when he and his friends would sneak away from their responsibilities. They would throw rocks into the nearby lake, watching the ripples spread and distort their reflections, or chase hares through the woods, their laughter echoing amongst the trees. Those fleeting moments of freedom, so scarce and precious, now returned to him with a vivid clarity.

The path wound down into the woods, the canopy of leaves creating a subtle pattern of light and shadow on the ground. The birds chirped merrily in the trees, their songs weaving a melody of peace and simplicity. A nearby stream babbled, its clear waters tumbling over rocks and roots, its soothing sound a balm to his troubled spirit.

For the first time in what felt like forever, the Cleric allowed himself to be fully present in the moment, to take in the beauty and tranquillity of nature around him. The weight of his usual responsibilities, the constant pressure of his role within the Order, seemed to lift away, replaced by an almost childlike sense of wonder.

Yet, beneath this veneer of tranquillity, a darker purpose lurked. The Cleric was not on a mere walk of reminiscence or escape; he had a mission, one that carried grave consequences. The Cleric had a new purpose.

He was here to destroy them all.

The thought, though chilling, did not waver his resolve.

This path he walked now, both literal and figurative, was one of no return. The Cleric understood the magnitude of what he was about to do, the irreversible impact of his actions. Yet, he felt a strange sense of peace, a conviction that his course was just, that the ends would justify the means.

As he moved deeper into the woods, his thoughts shifted from the past to the present, from memories of innocent freedom to the grim reality of his task. The sounds of the birds and running stream seemed to fade into the background, overshadowed by the gravity of his mission.

He paused for a moment, taking a deep breath of the fresh, woodland air. This could very well be the last time he experienced such peace, such simple beauty. With a final look at the serene world around him, he steeled himself and continued on his path.

What lay ahead was a task of darkness. He would do what needed to be done, for the sake of the world and all goodness.

26

DELIA

Delia sat at her kitchen counter, sunshine streaming in from the window, a cup of coffee steaming gently in her hands. Kitty was just tidying up the breakfast things after Delia had cooked them eggs benedict. The world outside seemed to be waking up from its winter slumber, with the freshness of spring in the air.

There was a soft knock at the door.

Delia set down her coffee and walked to the door to find Marjie's familiar face peering in through the side window.

"Come in," Delia said warmly.

Marjie entered, bringing with her a comforting presence. "Good morning, Delia! I thought I'd pop by for a bit," she said with a rosy smile.

"I'm just having a coffee. Would you like some tea?" she offered, already moving towards the kitchen.

"That would be lovely," Marjie replied, greeting Kitty and settling down at the kitchen table.

As Delia prepared tea, the quiet of the morning settled around them, comfortable and familiar.

Kitty finished the dishes and then excused herself to go and read upstairs.

The kettle whistled, and soon Marjie and Delia were both cradling warm mugs, the aroma of tea and coffee mingling in the air.

The conversation flowed easily between them, like it always did, but there was something on Delia's mind, a weight that seemed to tug at her words. After a pause, she took a deep breath and looked at Marjie. "I need to talk to you about something...It's about Declan."

Marjie's expression softened, her eyes filled with understanding. "Of course. What's on your mind, dear?"

Delia hesitated, her fingers wrapped tightly around her mug. "It's just...I don't know what to think. I have these feelings for him, but he's gone away now. And I know so little about him," she confessed, her voice tinged with confusion and a hint of sadness. "I can't talk to Kitty about it without being teased, and I wanted a more sympathetic ear."

Marjie reached across the table, offering a reassuring touch. "Delia, it's okay to be confused. Feelings can be complicated, especially when there's such uncertainty involved."

Delia nodded, a small smile tugging at her lips. "I hoped to have a chance to figure things out with Declan, but he left. I just wish I knew what was going on with him, or if...if he'll even come back." She sighed. "I wish I didn't feel like a limerent teenager! I thought I was over all that nonsense."

Marjie leaned back, her gaze thoughtful. "From what I've seen, the way he looks at you...I'd be surprised if he could stay away for long. There's something there, Delia. I can see it."

"There's something...certainly," said Delia. "But the lack of clarity is giving me vertigo."

"Oh love, it's hard isn't it? Having these feelings, even at our ages!" Marjie smiled empathetically. "But whatever happens, remember, you're not alone. We're here for you."

Delia sipped her coffee, the warmth from the mug spreading through her fingers. "How have things been with you and Papa Jack?" she asked, changing the subject.

Marjie sighed, stirring her tea absentmindedly. "He's been wrapped up with family stuff, and I've been busy with all my things. We've hardly seen much of each other lately," she admitted with a slight shrug. "Although I did pop in for a chat at the chocolate shop the other day and he was as supportive as ever – especially about trying to contact my brother."

"No change there?" Delia prompted.

Marjie shook her head sadly. "He still isn't returning my calls. Papa Jack keeps encouraging me to take more decisive action, but I can't very well just pop on a train to Yorkshire. What excuse do I have to barge in on him?"

Delia's brow furrowed. "Excuse me for a moment," she said, standing up. She stepped out to the hall, pulling out her phone. Her fingers moved frantically as she searched for something. A few taps later, she was making a quick call, her voice low.

She returned to the kitchen a moment later, a mysterious smile playing on her lips.

Marjie looked up, curiosity piqued. "What's that mischievous look about?"

Delia took her seat again, the smile still lingering. "Well, it just so happens that I have an appointment in Yorkshire with a certain accountant next Tuesday," she revealed. "I don't suppose you'd join me?"

Marjie's jaw dropped. "You didn't!"

"I'm afraid I did," Delia admitted with a glint in her eye. "I can cancel if you want me to, but this could be the easiest way to see your brother and hopefully get our hands on that family grimoire of yours. What do you think?"

Marjie took a deep breath. "I tend to trust my gut on these things," she said after a moment. "And even though it's fluttering with nervous butterflies right now, I think we're on the right track. Thank you, Delia. You're a good friend," she added, her eyes sparkling with gratitude and a hint of excitement.

The morning sun seemed to shine a little brighter.

27
MARJIE

Marjie sighed and took another sip of tea from her thermos as she took in the scenic beauty of rolling hills and quaint villages blurring past the car window. Delia's steady grip on the steering wheel and occasional glances of encouragement were the only anchors in Marjie's stormy contemplation. Her thoughts were a turbulent sea, churning with apprehension, old grief, and unresolved emotions.

The conversation had been stilted. Marjie didn't know what to say.

The closer they got, the tighter the knot in Marjic's stomach twisted. It was a long drive; they'd left early in the morning and stopped several times along the way.

Delia had tried to lighten the mood by suggesting they take a few nice strolls and stop for cake, but either the food was terribly bland or Marjie's emotional state kept her from tasting it, just as she wasn't able to enjoy the countryside they passed.

By the time they reached the small town south of York where Graham's accounting office apparently was, Marjie was wound so tightly she thought she might very well burst into magic dust in the air.

When Delia's warm hand squeezed hers, it was a much-needed gesture of support. Marjie offered a weak smile in response, her voice barely audible as she expressed her gratitude for Delia's help.

Marjie's heart raced as they neared Graham's office. Memories, long buried, surfaced like ghosts from the past. Each one was a reminder of the pain and estrangement that had grown over the years. She found herself gripping the edge of her seat, her knuckles white, as if bracing for an impact. *Can I really face him?*

Stepping into the building, Marjie's legs began to tremble. The receptionist's smile seemed to stretch too wide, doing little to ease the tension that buzzed in Marjie's ears.

Graham's office was stark, the minimalistic decor a reflection of the man himself. When they entered, Graham stood. "Delia, I presume? And you must be...?" His gaze landed on Marjie, shock flaring in his eyes briefly before he donned a mask of professional detachment.

"It's me, Marjie, Graham. It's been..." Marjie's voice trailed off to barely a whisper as she and Delia took their seats in front of Graham's large glass desk.

Graham's eyes narrowed ever so slightly, the corners of his mouth tightening. "Indeed. What brings you here?"

Marjie's fingers twisted in her lap, a silent battle raging within her. She raised her head, meeting Graham's gaze with a newfound resolve. "I've been trying to ring you for weeks," she stated, her voice gaining strength. "You haven't answered any of my calls..."

"I've been busy," he said, eyes downcast.

"It's been a long time, Graham," Marjie said, her voice laced with a sadness that hinted at years of disconnect.

"Too long," Graham replied, giving Marjie the faintest flicker of hope. She was sure she could see a trace of regret in his eyes.

The conversation was stilted, Graham's replies short and guarded.

Delia, clearly sensing the rising tension, gently guided the topic toward the grimoire. "Graham, Marjie mentioned a family grimoire. It would mean a lot to her to have it," Delia said, her voice a calm force in the room.

Graham's response hardened, his gaze flicking between the two women. "I don't see how that's any of your concern," he replied, his voice a cold blade slicing the air.

Marjie felt the sting of his words, the room seemingly shrinking around her. Here sat her brother, yet the gulf between them felt wider than the Yorkshire moors. She wished then that their mission was nothing more than a quest for an artifact rather than a poor attempt to bridge a familial gap that time and bitterness had eroded beyond recognition.

Graham suddenly stood up, his expression unreadable. "Excuse me for a moment, I need to make a call," he said abruptly, leaving the room with his phone in hand. The door clicked shut behind him, leaving Delia and Marjie in a tense silence.

Delia glanced at Marjie, who was staring at the closed door.

"What do you think he's doing?" Delia whispered.

Marjie shrugged, her eyes not leaving the door. "I have no idea. With Graham, it's hard to tell."

Several minutes dragged on, each one stretching out longer than the last. The office, with its sterile decor, felt even more unwelcoming now. Delia fidgeted with her purse, while Marjie folded and unfolded a corner of her coat, both lost in their thoughts.

Finally, the door opened, and Graham reappeared, his expression inscrutable. He sat down, clasping his hands on the desk.

"I've thought about it," he began, his voice carefully neutral. "I'm willing to discuss the grimoire. Let's meet tomorrow evening. There's a hotel restaurant in York where we can talk more privately."

Marjie felt her eyes widen in surprise. "Thank you, Graham," she replied with as much warmth as she could muster. "We'll be there."

As Marjie and Delia left the office, the air outside seemed fresher, less oppressive. Marjie took a deep breath, looking up at the sky. "I didn't expect that," she said, a hint of a smile touching her lips.

Delia nodded. "Tomorrow could change everything," she said.

Back in the safety of the car, Marjie let out a sigh, her shoulders sagging slightly. "That was harder than I thought," she admitted. "But I'm glad we did it. It's a start, at least."

Delia nodded. "It's good progress, Marjie. I don't want to alarm you, but we must be prepared for the worst."

"What do you mean exactly?" Marjie asked. "He's already ignored my calls. Agreeing to meet us is a great step forward, isn't it?"

Delia sighed. "Oh, Marjie, I hate to even bring this up, but don't you think Graham was behaving suspiciously? As if he had something to hide?"

Marjie shrugged. "That's just his way."

Delia reached over and patted her on the shoulder. "And I really hope there's nothing else to it, and my paranoia is unfounded," Delia continued. "But there could be a chance that something underhanded is going on here. We have to be prepared."

Marjie smiled. "That's my personal motto, don't you worry!"

28
DELIA

Delia scanned the room as she navigated through the bustling pub, Marjie in tow. Graham had called this a restaurant, but it was more of a pub in Delia's view. The din of voices and clinking glasses enveloped them. The air was warm and heavy with the scent of ale and fried food.

"There he is!" said Marjie, tugging at Delia's sleeve.

"Where?" Delia's eyes finally landed on Graham.

He was sitting alone in a booth, wiping his brow with a handkerchief, both hands trembling. His previously well-composed demeanour was nowhere to be seen; instead, he looked like a man under immense pressure.

This is bad...

Marjie's brows furrowed in concern as she took in her brother's state.

Delia didn't want to frighten Marjie any further, but something was clearly wrong and they needed to figure out what it was as quickly as possible.

As they approached, Graham's gaze flicked nervously around the room before settling on them. He attempted a smile, but it didn't quite reach his eyes.

Delia greeted him, sliding into the booth with as much cheer as she could muster in the noisy pub.

"Hi, Graham." Marjie followed, sitting opposite her brother, her hands clasped tightly in her lap with a tight smile plastered on her face.

“Hello,” he replied.

“This is a busy pub, isn’t it? I bet the food’s good,” Marjie said, overly cheerful, clearly hoping to break the tension.

“I s’pose,” said Graham.

"So, Graham, how have you been?" she asked, her attempt at casual conversation feeling forced in the charged atmosphere.

Graham shifted uncomfortably, his eyes darting around the room before landing on his sister. "Busy," he replied curtly.

Marjie nodded, though the answer clearly offered her little satisfaction. "I've been trying to reach you," she pressed on, her tone tinged with hope and frustration. "I’ve...missed you."

Graham's response was a noncommittal grunt.

Delia chimed in, trying to ease the tension. "This pub has a great vibe, doesn't it? I love the energy here." Her words felt hollow in her own ears, an inadequate bandage over a gaping wound.

"Yeah, it's fine," Graham muttered, his attention clearly

elsewhere. He took a sip of his drink, his hand trembling slightly.

Delia exchanged a glance with Marjie.

"So, Graham, any plans for the weekend?" Marjie ventured again, her voice a mixture of hopefulness and desperation.

"No," he said. "No plans."

The conversation was so awkward and fragmented that Delia's anxiety began to rise. She breathed a sigh of relief that her powers were much more firmly under control now, lest her heightened state set the whole place on fire. The mostly-full glasses on the table trembled though. Marjie was clearly having a hard time keeping her magic in check. This situation wouldn't be helped by the emotional turmoil emanating so strongly from Graham. Even Delia could barely stand to stay in the conversation which was drowned out occasionally by the raucous laughter and chatter surrounding them.

Delia tried to prompt Graham to explain why he'd asked to meet them there, but his answers were evasive, his eyes darting around the room, sweat beading on his forehead.

Marjie seemed lost, her attempts at bridging the gap with her brother faltering with each monosyllabic response he gave.

"Don't you remember the pub in Myrtlewood, Graham?" Marjie asked. "We used to have dinner there on Saturday nights once a month as a treat – the whole family."

Graham's expression softened. "I remember," he said gently.

Delia's suspicions that Graham was trying to trick them melted when she saw the genuine expression of sadness and warmth on his face. But if he wasn't there to trap them or sabotage their attempt to retrieve the grimoire, then something else was going on.

She began scanning the room, trying to piece together the puzzle of Graham's unusual behavior.

Her gaze landed on a solitary figure at the bar – his posture too stiff, his glances too calculated. Something about him screamed 'Order of Crimson', and a chill ran down her spine. She leaned in closer to Graham, lowering her voice to be heard over the din.

"Graham, I know we've just met, but I'm going to assume you're not quite yourself, lately," she said softly. "Is there undue stress? Something we should know about?"

Graham's eyes flickered to Delia, then to the figure at the bar, and back. He nodded almost imperceptibly. The confirmation was subtle, but Delia caught it, a silent alarm bell ringing in her head.

The realisation that Graham was possibly under surveillance from the Order changed everything. Delia exchanged a quick, significant glance with Marjie, communicating a world of warning without words.

Marjie, gathering her courage, leaned forward slightly, her eyes searching her brother's face. "Graham, about the family grimoire..."

Graham's reaction was immediate and telling. He shook his head sharply, cutting her off mid-sentence. His eyes briefly flashed with fear.

Marjie's face fell, disappointment clouding her features.

She opened her mouth as if to protest, but then seemed to think better of it, her shoulders slumping in defeat.

Delia, however, was watching closely, her instincts telling her that there was more to Graham's reaction.

She caught Marjie's eye, giving her a small, reassuring nod. It was a silent communication to trust her, to let the matter of the grimoire lie for now. Marjie, though visibly frustrated, seemed to understand, taking a deep breath and nodding in return.

"You asked us to come here for a reason, didn't you, Graham," said Delia, her voice quiet.

He nodded subtly and Marjie's shoulders relaxed slightly next to Delia.

"And you know why Marjie needed to come here. You know why we came to see you," Delia continued.

Graham nodded again.

"It's loud in here," said Delia, looking around again. The man at the bar turned his head sharply as she caught sight of him. Delia turned back and lowered her voice. "You don't feel safe talking, I get that, but what is it—"

"I need another drink," Graham said abruptly.

"Okay..." Delia began, in confusion.

Graham caught her hand and pulled her closer. "Go up to the bar, both of you, wait for a minute and then sneak out through the crowd. He won't see you leave. He'll be watching me and I'll distract him."

"But..." Delia shot Marjie a concerned glance, but as Graham squeezed her hand she felt something warm, soft, and slightly damp, pressed into her palm.

"Go now," he said, with sorrowful eyes locked on Marjie's. "And I hope to see you again soon. I really do."

"Graham," Marjie said, as she and Delia got up from the table.

"I'm sorry," his voice croaked out. "Just go."

29
DECLAN

Declan materialised in the shadow of an ancient oak, the dark night air heavy with the scent of rain and earth. He had been leading the Order on a relentless chase, and now he was close to their base, again, with the intent of taunting them once more. The compound of the Order of Crimson loomed in the distance, its silhouette stark against the moonlit sky, enchanted so that most eyes would simply slip over it, but Declan's practiced gaze could see clearly. He took a deep breath and allowed himself a brief moment to gather his strength. He knew the Order's agents would be close on his heels.

He waited, the minutes dragging by, his senses sharp and attuned to the slightest sound. Then, he heard it – the rustle of leaves, the barely audible footsteps of his pursuers. Declan's heart pounded in his chest as he prepared himself.

With a swift, deliberate movement, Declan drew a portal, the shimmering gateway of magic opening before him. He stepped through and emerged in the middle of a bustling town square night market nearby, amid busy people who paid no attention to the appearance of a man from thin air, their rational minds simply explaining anything mysterious away. Declan scanned his surroundings, his eyes narrowing as he sensed the Order's changing tact. They had guards stationed here, and he had a vague idea where they might be.

He dashed through the narrow streets, his footfalls echoing in the night. Declan glanced over his shoulder to see dark figures emerging from the shadows, their pursuit relentless. He rounded a corner, his mind racing as he plotted his next move. With a quick flick of his wrist, another portal opened, and he dove through it, reappearing on the edge of a windswept cliff on the other side of the compound.

This new location afforded him a small rest, but the Order's agents soon appeared at the edge of the cliff. Declan could see the determination in their eyes as their red cloaks flapped in the wind, the unwavering intent to capture him. He stepped back, his heels teetering on the edge of the precipice, and with a grin, he activated yet another portal, this time appearing in the nearby forest.

The chase continued. He knew he was playing a dangerous game, but the longer he could keep the Order occupied, the more time Delia and the Crones had to secure their own safety. He emerged once again near the compound, his breath coming in ragged gasps. The agents were closing in, and Declan could feel the tension mounting.

Perhaps tonight he'd retreat back to Spain where the warmer air could soothe him into sleep, away from the

Order's grasp, yet also far away from the warmth he craved the most.

Suddenly, a searing pain shot through his side. He stumbled, glancing down to see a crimson stain spreading across his shirt. An arrow, tipped with poison, had found its mark. Declan gritted his teeth, his vision blurring as he struggled to stay upright. He couldn't afford to be caught now, not when so much was at stake.

The arrow would not kill him. He'd survived far worse. But he would not be captured, not now. Summoning his strength, Declan activated a new portal, collapsing backwards off the cliff as the Order's agents cried out.

He landed heavily on soft moss in a secluded grove. He lay there for a moment, panting, the pain in his side throbbing. He pulled the arrow from his side and the wound began to heal immediately. For so long, he would have cursed at this, hoping at last for an end and finding only a new beginning, but no longer.

Delia.

He needed to see her. To check she was safe. With trembling hands, he reached for the seer's stone, the cool surface of the crystal grounding him.

As the stone's light flared to life, Declan's vision cleared, revealing an image of Delia and Marjie.

His heart sank as he realised they were no longer in Myrtlewood. The familiar surroundings of Yorkshire framed them. Using the stone, he panned the nearby areas, honing in on the Order's agents. There they were, watching closely, plotting their next move.

A jolt of fear shot through Declan – his plan had worked well enough until now, but the Crones were up to something, and now that they'd drawn the Order's attention, his distractions would no longer be enough to keep them safe. He needed a new strategy, and something told him he'd be returning to Myrtlewood far sooner than he'd planned.

30
MARJIE

Marjie felt a knot of anticipation tighten in her stomach. The pre-dawn air was brisk as Marjie and Delia quietly slipped out of their hotel, their movements quick and purposeful. They'd tried to sleep, but had barely rested, and the early morning seemed like the best time for a dangerous mission.

They made their way through the darkness that enveloped the town like a shroud, the only light coming from the dim glow of distant street lamps.

"It was a good idea to cloak the lights," Delia whispered as they got into the car.

Marjie beamed at her. She'd worked up the spell just minutes ago so that all the nearby lights would go out to make their departure more stealthy. "What's the point in being a witch if you can't make a sneaky departure?"

Delia smiled back. "I'll remember that next time I'm stuck

at a boring party."

The stillness of the early morning lent an eerie calm to the atmosphere.

As Delia drove, the car's headlights cut through the darkness, casting long shadows on the road. Marjie gazed out the window, watching as the landscape gradually shifted from the sleepy town to the open countryside, and then to the awakening city of Leeds. The sky began to lighten, the first hints of dawn painting the horizon in soft hues of pink and orange.

Marjie's mind wandered to Graham, her thoughts a tangle of guilt and newfound understanding. "No wonder he never returned my calls," she mused aloud. "He was protecting me all this time."

Delia glanced at her with empathy. "We're all doing our best, Marjie. Be gentle with yourself, just like you're gentle with your friends."

"But I was so hard on Graham," Marjie said sadly.

"Family are the hardest sometimes, but give yourself a break and some compassion. You're the most caring person I know. If you judged Graham harshly, it was because you were afraid of his rejection."

Marjie let out a long sigh, Delia's words sinking in. "Isn't that the truth!"

She gazed out at the awakening city, a sense of resolve settling over her. Delia was right. Family could be the hardest people to deal with. Graham's actions, once a source of pain, were now evidence of his love and protection.

As they entered Leeds, the streets were mostly empty. The city was beginning to awaken but slowly, as if still rubbing sleep from its eyes. Puddles glistened on the pavement, reflecting the pale morning light, and the gutters were alive with the gentle rush of melting snow.

"Of course, it's possible that this is all a trap," Delia said cautiously. “Graham seemed genuine, and you would have felt his conflicted emotions more than me, but what if he’s conflicted because he’s leading us into danger?”

Marjie shook her head, dispelling the lingering doubt. "We can’t think like that," she replied. "It just doesn’t seem right. Now that I know he was trying to help...now that I've seen the sincere worry in his eyes, I can't bear to doubt him again."

As Delia and Marjie stepped out of the car, Marjie pulled her coat tighter around herself, the dampness seeping into her bones. They walked briskly and quietly, their footsteps a soft patter on the wet pavement. Marjie glanced around, her senses heightened.

“This is it,” Delia said.

As they approached the building in question, Marjie felt a flutter of nervous excitement. The structure loomed above them, its facade unassuming yet somehow imposing in the early light.

Delia led the way, her movements confident yet cautious. Marjie followed, her mind racing with possibilities. Could Graham really have outmanoeuvred the Order? Was the grimoire truly within their grasp?

They neared the entrance, Delia pausing to survey the area one last time before they entered. Marjie felt a surge of gratitude for her friend's calm and confident presence.

Marjie and Delia were mere steps away from the building

when the air in front of them shimmered, and a portal burst open with a violent crackle.

“No!” Marjie cried as three figures clad in red hoods emerged brandishing swords, their faces obscured, moving with swift, menacing intent.

"Watch out!" Delia shouted, pushing Marjie aside as the first attacker lunged forward.

Marjie stumbled back, her heart pounding. She saw Delia raise her hands. Flames erupted from her palms in a fiery whip that lashed out at the assailants.

“Nice!” Marjie called out. “A fire whip! I wonder if I could learn that.”

Delia shot her a grin. “I've been practicing. Get back!"

Marjie jumped backwards, regaining her balance, and looked around frantically. Her eyes landed on a nearby drain, water rushing through it from the melted snow. Instinctively, she extended her hands, muttering a spell under her breath. The water obeyed her call, swirling up and out of the drain, forming a swift, swirling vortex in her grasp.

"Take this!" Marjie cried, directing the torrent of drain water towards one of the attackers. The force of the water hit him square in the chest, sending him sprawling back into the portal. "Delia, behind you!" she screamed, as the third figure lunged forwards.

Delia spun around, her fire magic exploding in a burst of heat and light. The attacker recoiled, the hood falling back to reveal a twisted snarl of anger.

“I don't know why you bother disguising yourselves,” Delia said. “You all look the same to me, masked or not. That's the problem with you Order lot, you're all conformists – there's nothing original about you. Take that message back to my ex-husband and tell him to get some new ideas."

Marjie crowed with laughter, dropping her guard for a moment too long. The attacker she'd held with her magic recovered and began chanting over his sword, which glowed with a creepy red light. "This blade will remove your magic you foolish old woman!"

Marjie chuckled as she blasted him with more water, using the chill of his own fear to freeze it into ice. He cried out and the blade clattered to the ground.

"That's fabulous old woman to you," she said, with a hand on her hip.

The fight was chaotic, a blur of motion, magic, and shouts. Marjie's heart raced as she ducked and weaved, her water spell drenching another attacker. Delia was a whirlwind of fiery fury.

Finally, with a concerted effort, Delia sent a massive blast of fire towards the attackers, while Marjie's water vortex engulfed them; her hands moved in intricate patterns as she chanted under her breath. The attackers, disoriented and defeated, found themselves suddenly bound by her spell, their limbs locked in place as if held by invisible ropes. They lay in a tangled pile, groaning and struggling against the magical restraints.

Marjie and Delia stood there for a moment, catching their breath, their eyes wide with the adrenaline of the fight. "That was fun...but a little too close for comfort," Marjie gasped.

Delia nodded. "We have to be careful. The Order is onto us."

"But do they know why we're here?" Marjie asked. "Or did they just use a spell to locate us? We are out of the protective barrier of Myrtlewood, after all."

Delia shrugged. "Let's hope they have no idea. The less they know, the better."

"How do we get in?" Marjie asked, motioning towards the building.

Delia walked forward and the glass in front of her glided to both sides.

The Order members gasped as they lay on the footpath, still tangled and bound.

"What magic is this?" Marjie asked.

Delia chuckled. "You don't get out much, do you? These are your standard mundane sliding doors – powered through electricity."

"Well, they don't have these in Myrtlewood," said Marjie. "Blooming convenient, though, aren't they? Maybe I could get some for the teashop."

"How do you know any pop culture references at all if you don't know what sliding doors are?" Delia asked, narrowing her eyes.

"I hardly watch the telly. I don't even have one," Marjie said, seeming more herself than she had since they'd first started the trip. "But the young ones come and show me all kinds of things on their phones, don't they? Last summer, young Felix tried to convince me that Mervyn was secretly a buff movie star. I almost believed him!"

Delia chuckled as they slipped into the building. The walls were lined with steel, neatly set into square shapes.

Marjie watched, a mixture of awe and disbelief, as Delia approached a screen and entered the code from the napkin Graham had given them at the pub. He had slipped it into her hand and Delia had taken it, not realising what the soft damp thing was until they were safely back at their hotel where she and Marjie had opened it up to discover simple directions and a line of numbers scrawled hastily onto the cheap crimped paper.

With a series of beeps, the machine whirred to life, and a metal box slid open, revealing a package wrapped in brown paper.

"Remarkable!" Marjie exclaimed, her eyes wide. The simplicity of it all, hidden behind a facade of complexity, was almost laughable.

She reached out and took the package, feeling a warm tingle run through her fingers as she touched it. "Do you want to check it first?" Delia asked, her eyes curious.

"No," Marjie replied, clutching the package close to her chest. "It feels right. Let's just get out of here!"

They left the building in haste, Marjie's heart pounding.

As they passed the pile of Order members, one of them managed to gasp out, "They have it! What magic held the sacred relic? We've been trying to crack it for weeks, ever since we followed that wretched man here!"

Delia couldn't help but laugh. "Simple electricity and a computer system."

They reached the car, Marjie glancing back one last time at the immobilised figures. "How clever of Graham," she muttered, still clutching the grimoire to her chest. "He would have realised he didn't have the magic to hide this from them, but he also had the insight to reason that an ancient magical cult would know very little about modern technology."

"And he did this to protect you," Delia said as she started the engine and pulled away.

Marjie felt a wave of relief wash over her. "That's true. Graham could have simply given the sacred family treasure to the Order. He's hated magic all these years. I would have thought he'd be glad to be rid of the thing."

"But he clearly cares about you," Delia said gently. "And he's clever enough to know that the book was important – both to you and to them. He could have asked them for money or power, they would have tried to bribe him and threaten him, but he chose you."

The warmth spreading through Marjie's chest melted the icy shell she'd built up around her heart to protect her from the pain in her own family. "That's right. He chose me. And he'd better get used to having me in his life again, because as soon as he's out of danger he's going to be seeing a lot more of me!"

Delia smiled at her. "Now where shall we stop for breakfast?"

"Somewhere with good pancakes," said Marjie. "I bet you even have technology to figure out where that might be."

"I certainly I do," Delia said.

Marjie's heart soared as the sun rose higher in the sky. They had the grimoire, they had outsmarted the Order, and now they were on their way home with the promise of pancakes on the way, and perhaps even mended family bonds in her future.

31
DELIA

Back in Myrtlewood, the familiar comfort of home wrapped around Delia like a warm embrace. She descended the stairs to the aroma of pancakes cooking – a sure sign that Kitty was already up and about, preparing for the day.

In the kitchen, Kitty stood at the stove, expertly flipping pancakes, her movements graceful and practiced. Delia moved towards the coffee pot, pouring herself a steaming cup, the rich scent of the brew bringing a small, comforting smile to her face.

Today was special – her grandkids, Merryn and Keyne, were due to visit. The thought brought both excitement and a twinge of anxiety. She hadn't seen them in a while, and their visits were always a bright spot in her life.

As she sipped her coffee, the sound of a car pulling up outside caught her attention. She peered out the window, expecting to see her daughter, Gillian, but instead, she saw an unfamiliar car. The door opened, and Merryn and Keyne tumbled out, waving goodbye to the driver before running towards the house.

Delia's heart sank slightly at the absence of Gillian. She couldn't help but worry about her daughter, wondering why she hadn't come. Gilly had been curt and hurried over the phone, and Delia knew something strange was going on, she only wished she knew the details. But as the children burst through the door, their faces alight with excitement, she pushed her concerns aside, replacing them with a bright, welcoming smile.

"Nanna!" they chorused, throwing themselves into her arms.

Delia hugged them tightly, feeling their youthful energy and unconditional love. "I've missed you both so much!" she exclaimed, her heart swelling with affection.

"Look how much you've grown!" she marvelled, holding them at arm's length to get a better look. Merryn's hair was longer, and Keyne had a new-found confidence in his eyes.

As they chatted animatedly about their journey and all the things they wanted to do during their visit, Delia listened, her smile unwavering. But in the back of her mind, she couldn't shake her concern for Gillian. She made a mental note to call her later, to check in and make sure everything was alright.

For now, though, she would focus on the joy of having her grandchildren around, filling the house with laughter and life. She ushered them into the kitchen where Kitty had a stack of pancakes ready, the table set for a feast.

"Pancakes!" Keyne exclaimed, his eyes lighting up.

"Your favourite," Kitty said, winking at him.

As they all sat down to eat, the worries of the world seemed to melt away, replaced by the simple pleasure of family and the warmth of shared moments. Delia sipped her coffee, watching her grandchildren with a heart full of love, silently vowing to do whatever it took to keep them safe and happy.

A short while later, Merryn and Keyne chattered in excitement as they entered the bustling town hall where the Myrtlewood Players were gathering for rehearsal. The group was a vibrant mish mash of local talent, each member buzzing with the anticipation of trying out scenes from Ash's new script.

"Who's ready for games?" Delia announced, her voice carrying over the chatter. The children's eyes lit up with excitement, their earlier apprehension melting away in the warmth of the room.

They repeated some of Delia's favourite warm ups, the children joining in, delightedly. Laughter and cheers filled the hall.

Merryn and Keyne watched, wide-eyed, as Ferg, the Mayor, added his own dramatic flair to the games, his bright orange robe swirling with each exaggerated motion.

"You're quite the performer, Ferg," Delia teased, her laughter mingling with the group's. "Now, it's time to read from the script," she continued. "Who wants to go first? And let me know afterwards if there's a particular part you're interested in."

Merryn and Keyne sat at the front, their faces a picture of awe and delight as they watched the adults transform into their characters.

Delia had read and thoroughly enjoyed the script. In fact,

she had relatively few suggestions, and Ash lit up when she praised her writing.

As the excitement continued to swell, Delia gathered everyone around for the next scene. "Let's try the confrontation between the Cailleach and the Winter King. Obviously we're not assigning any parts yet, this is just to get a feel for the play. For now, Ferg, you'll read for the Cailleach, and Sid, take the part of the King."

Ferg stepped forward, his bright robe adding to his already commanding presence. Sid, usually confident as the head of the fire department, looked a bit nervous but took her place.

"Remember," Delia advised, "these are powerful gods. Let the power of these elements flow through you."

"Winter's grip shall not be broken," Ferg intoned, his voice deep and resonant.

"But spring's light will always return," Sid responded, then frowned, breaking character. “This isn’t right. I can’t get into character.”

Delia shrugged. “Let me try.”

She picked up the script and read with Sid, taking the part Ferg had previously read. Delia concentrated and surrendered to the flow of words and emotion. She’d only meant to read a line or two, but they got carried away, lost in the magic of performance. Delia found herself wrapped up in the role of Cailleach, as if she’d fully embraced and embodied the goddess’s wintery energy. Sid responded by gracefully sliding into Brigid’s character, becoming radiant and confident as she read.

As the scene came to a natural end, the entire group broke into spontaneous applause.

"That...was amazing," said Sid. "I've never been so enthralled in a role before." She narrowed her eyes at Delia. "You're a powerful theatre witch."

Delia cackled. "I'm more of a fire witch, I'm afraid. And more of a director than an actor."

"Don't be so sure," said Ferg. "That performance was sensational. I've never seen anything like it."

Delia shook her head. "It's a good script, that's all."

"No," Ferg said firmly. "It's more than that. I'll show you." He pointed to Sherry. "Read from the top of page six with me."

He and Sherry began to read lines together, fumbling through in a fairly ordinary way as far as new scripts went.

"What's your point?" Delia asked.

"Wait," said Ferg. "Now you read with me, Delia."

Delia sighed and began to read from the same page, only this time, Ferg transformed as he read the lines of the spring goddess, drawing himself fully into character, charming and lively.

Applause erupted once more as they finished the scene.

Delia looked around, perplexed. "You did that, Ferg. You acted so well."

Ferg shook his head. "No, you did. Something about you drew me into the scene. It's powerful magic."

Delia shrugged. "I'm not really an actor."

Painful memories from the fatal moment in her acting career careened in her mind.

"We need you to act with us," Ferg insisted.

Delia shook her head. "I won't do it."

His shoulders slumped in disappointment.

"Delia," Kitty said, gesturing from the back of the room. "Can I talk to you for just a moment?"

"Sure, let's take a break," Delia said to the others, then joined Kitty at the back of the room. "What is it?"

"You're not going to wriggle out of this one, is all," said Kitty, with a sly smile.

"What do you mean?" Delia asked.

"That pompous fellow was right – your acting brought out the best in him, and the tall woman."

Delia shook her head. "I'm not here to act. I'm just helping out."

"You're scared," said Kitty. "Look at you, you're practically trembling."

Delia looked down at her shaky hands and tried to still them. "So what?"

"So, I'm here to tell you that you really have to do this. You're a brilliant actor, Delia, you've just been hiding from your failure all these years, which is understandable, but it's not who you are. You're a brave woman. And besides, it was your awful ex who engineered that failure to manipulate you. Don't keep giving your power away to that man."

Delia turned her back to the room and covered her face with her hands, blinking into her palms for a moment. Kitty's words had struck a chord, but that didn't mean she had to act, did it? Surely she could simply accept her friend's point and get on with other things. As she stood there, her head slightly bowed in the darkness created by her hands, Kitty continued talking.

"I had to talk to you just now, I just had a feeling about it, because something big is happening here, and I don't want you to miss it," Kitty said, putting her hand on Delia's shoulder.

"I can't do it," Delia mumbled. "Besides, this isn't anything big, it's just community theatre."

"Then what are you so afraid of?" Kitty asked. "I'm sure these people fall flat on their face all the time!"

Delia supressed an involuntary laugh and removed her hands, blinking into the light.

"But it is big," Kitty continued. "It's big for you. You need to get back on the horse. You didn't do it all those years ago, you took a different path rather than facing your own shame, and now you have a new opportunity – in a group of quirky, friendly oddballs. The stakes are low, so why don't you let yourself shine like you were always meant to do?"

"Nanna!" Keyne called enthusiastically as the children rushed over holding berry muffins from the array of snacks people had brought to share.

"You were brilliant," said Merryn. "Are you going to be in the play?"

Delia took a deep breath. "I don't know, darling. It's been a very long time since I was in a play."

"But you're so good at it," Merryn continued. "It would be a shame not to."

"Yes," Keyne added. "It would be very sad because this is a golden opportunity."

Delia smiled at them. "Is that right?"

The children nodded enthusiastically.

"Well..." Delia leaned in towards them. "To tell you the truth, I'm scared to be up on stage in the limelight."

"I can understand that, Nanna," said Merryn with a maturity beyond her years, as if she'd faced many such obstacles herself. "But it really would be so good if you did it anyway. Besides, you tell us not to be scared, when you're tucking us in at night. There's nothing to be frightened of."

Keyne gave Delia a knowing look. "Sometimes you just have to be brave, Nanna."

Delia felt her cheeks flush. The children were right, Kitty was right...as much as she hated to admit it. She could feel the fear like a band around her chest, constricting her, holding her back, keeping her safe, and yet, she would be far safer on the small stage than in many other situations she'd been in since starting her new magical life. Perhaps even the burning threat of shame was nothing to fear. She sighed deeply, then she smiled at her grandchildren. "Well, I'll have to see what the rest of the group thinks, but perhaps I'll give acting another go, after all."

32
MARJIE

In the warm kitchen of Thorn Manor, Marjie sat at the old oak table, a pot of steaming tea beside her. The retrieved grimoire lay open, its leather-bound cover cracked with age, a memoir of the generations of her family who had created it and turned its pages over the centuries. The morning light streamed through the window.

The weight of the book in her hands was a physical link to her heritage, a connection both profound and bittersweet. The pages were worn, the ink faded in places, but each word was a connection, a stitch in the fabric that bound her to her ancestors.

As Marjie leafed through the pages, a sense of connection to her family's past enveloped her. The marginalia, scribbled in various hands, spoke of daily life and magical discoveries. A note in the margin of a potion recipe for calming nerves, written in her grandmother's elegant script, brought a smile to her face: "Perfect for pre-ritual jitters."

As she turned the pages, Marjie smiled, making a note to contact Graham as soon as it was safe to do so. They could reminisce about their family history and properly reconnect after the danger had passed.

Marjie smiled to herself as she read a snarky comment about a spell's effectiveness, and then a gentler warning about a particularly tricky potion – each note was a conversation across time.

Another page revealed a recipe for a hearty stew, the ingredients listed in a firm, practical hand. Beside it, a relative had added a note: "Mum's favourite on cold winter nights. Never fails to warm the heart and soul." Marjie could almost smell the stew simmering on the stove, the aroma mingling with the scent of her English Breakfast tea.

One page was folded at the corner, and Marjie frowned as she unfolded it, wondering who had mistreated this special book. But here, she discovered an old family recipe for a healing salve, the handwriting elegant and precise. "For wounds and aches of all kinds," the note beside it read, in her great-grandmother's script. Marjie could almost hear the woman's voice, stern yet caring, echoing through the years. She made a mental note to make the salve as it would no doubt be useful.

Further along, sandwiched between two different sponge cake recipes – each proclaiming to be better than the other – she found detailed instructions on how to harvest the energy of the moon to enhance intuition.

Flicking further through the book, she discovered sketches of rare herbs and plants, their uses detailed in meticulous handwriting. Each annotation was a whisper from the past, connecting her to the lineage of strong, resilient individuals who had shaped her destiny.

This book contained much wisdom, yes, but it wasn't just the knowledge that captivated Marjie; it was the personal touches, the human element that shone through. A smudge of ink where someone had rested their hand, a hastily scribbled note about a spell gone awry – these were reminders that the grimoire had been a living part of her family, a constant companion through joy and sorrow.

Tucked between the pages were pressed flowers, their colours faded but still beautiful. Marjie ran her fingers over them gently, imagining her ancestors tending their gardens, finding solace among the blooms.

As she delved deeper, Marjie found herself smiling at a child's drawing tucked between the pages – a crude depiction of a witch in front of a cauldron, the word "Mama" scrawled underneath. She couldn't remember if it was from her generation – perhaps she or Graham or even Jowell had drawn it – or perhaps it was created by a child in her father's generation. Either way it was a reminder of the family that had once been closely knit, of a time before tragedy and estrangement had taken their toll.

The grimoire was not just a collection of spells and wisdom; it was a family album, a chronicle of a journey through the ages. With each page, Marjie felt a growing sense of connection, not just to her magical heritage, but to the people who had made it. The sadness of her family's past mingled with a newfound hope.

Marjie wiped away her tears of sadness, happiness, and longing, as she heard footsteps approaching.

A moment later Rosemary Thorn entered the kitchen quietly. A gentle smile graced her lips.

"How are you this morning, Marjie?" Rosemary asked as she moved to join her at the table.

"Better than I could have imagined," she replied, her voice warm with appreciation. "Who'd have thought a book could hold so much emotion – joy and nostalgia, and all!"

Rosemary's smile widened. "Any clues?" she inquired gently, her gaze drifting over the open pages. "Now that I know about your Crone secrets, I want all the goss."

Marjie chuckled and shook her head. "It might be easier to find clues about the Crones if I knew the book well, but unfortunately, I never had the pleasure. Agatha and Ingrid had their grimoires for decades and knew them inside and out, which meant that their awakened powers revealed extra information to them which they could tell apart from what was already there. My father only let us look at this book occasionally when we were growing up, but this is a treasure trove all the same."

Rosemary reached out, her fingers brushing the edge of the grimoire. "It's more than a book, isn't it?"

Marjie nodded, her eyes returning to the pages. "Exactly. It's like rediscovering a part of myself I didn't realise was missing. And it's helping me understand my family in ways I never did before."

The two friends sat in comfortable silence, occasionally

smiling or laughing over a detail in the grimoire as Marjie turned the pages to discover more treasures. As usual, Marjie felt a sense of peace in Rosemary's company, a reminder that while the past was important, it was the present – and the people in it – that truly enriched her life.

33
THE SHEPHERD

Father Benedict paced the compound, power surging through him as he restored order everywhere he looked. The very stones beneath his feet seeming to yield to his will. The Elders, those stalwart defenders of tradition, were bound and out of the way, their authority crumbling in the face of the Almighty's ascent.

Their fear is a shackle they have forged for themselves, the voice spoke in his mind, the voice of the Almighty, carrying the weight of unshakeable conviction.

The Shepherd's eyes, sharp and penetrating, scanned the ancient tapestries that adorned the corridors, depicting Order's storied past. "But I...I have been unshackled. The Almighty has shown me the way forward, a path they are too blind to see."

As he walked, Father Benedict's mind swirled with visions of the future he would forge. The old ways would be cast aside, replaced by a new order born of his divine purpose.

The Elders' time had passed, their schemes mere shadows against the brilliance of his plan.

They do not understand, the powerful voice of the Almighty snaked through his mind. *Even now, disempowered and bound, they scheme against us.*

"Let them scheme," Benedict said, a sly smile curling the edges of his lips. "Their desperation only serves to highlight their weakness. They cling to a past that is already fading into the shadows."

As he strode around the compound, waving his arms majestically, the deep and powerful magic of the Almighty poured out of him. Every crack in the masonry trembled and repaired itself, every weed drawing through the stone pathways wilted and receded.

With each step The Shepherd took, the Order of Crimson transformed further, the Almighty's magic weaving through the corridors like a dark army marching in battle.

The walls shimmered around him and pulsed, ancient stone yielding to the etchings of sacred symbols.

The monks, caught in the midst of their daily tasks, stopped in their tracks, their eyes wide with awe and fear. They watched as the disorderly piles of manuscripts and scrolls in the scriptorium lifted into the air, enveloped in a whirlwind of magic. Pages fluttered like wings of birds, aligning and organising themselves into neat, ordered stacks, before settling back onto the shelves, transformed into bound volumes of pristine condition.

As Father Benedict passed the dining hall, the clatter of dishes and cutlery ceased. Those who were eating paused mid-bite, watching as the tables and benches straightened and aligned themselves. Food that was scattered untidily rearranged itself on plates, looking more appealing and nourishing. The very cloaks they wore straightened and pressed themselves, as though offended by their own wrinkles.

In the gardens, vines and overgrown bushes recoiled and reshaped themselves, creating orderly patterns and clear walkways. The once wild thicket behind the salad beds now appeared as a meticulously crafted oasis of order.

Inside the chapel, candles burned with unwavering devotion, and stained glass windows cast kaleidoscopic light across the transformed space.

The very air within the Order's compound had changed – the musty odour of dust was gone. The ancient scent of stone and parchment now mingled with a new purity that suffused every corner.

With each manifestation of his will, Benedict's confidence grew. He moved with a purpose that was almost regal, his cloak trailing behind him. The dark tendrils of magic that extended from his fingertips were like the strings of a puppet master, reshaping the Order into a vision of divine perfection.

As the Order was reborn, Benedict's thoughts turned to the Crones and the challenges that lay ahead. Delia, once the core focus of his mission, was now a mere pawn to be swept aside. The tracker who hunted her would become an example of the price of disobedience.

He strode into the grand hall, his presence commanding

and his eyes alight with a newfound power. "Come now," he said, magnifying his voice so that it boomed through the entire compound. "Assemble."

Swiftly, guided by magic, the hall filled with all present members of the Order of Crimson.

"This is the dawn of a new era," he said, his voice compelling, inspiring and driving fear into the hearts of all those present. "I expect nothing but total obedience to the Almighty's will. No one will defy me."

Everyone present nodded.

"Where are my generals? Step forward."

The senior generals hesitated only a fraction of a second, but that did not escape the Shepherd's notice. They would have to be taught a lesson, but for now, he had something else to attend to.

"The tracker's punishment will be a spectacle," Benedict declared, his voice resonating through the hall. "A testament to the consequences of defying the Almighty's will."

The Almighty's power surged within him, a dark and intoxicating force that whispered promises of absolute dominion. Benedict's smile held a chilling edge as he envisioned the public display of the hunter's punishment, a demonstration that would strike fear into the hearts of all who witnessed it. As he contemplated his next move, a dark smile played upon Benedict's lips.

He imagined the scene vividly: the tracker, bound and helpless, brought before the assembled Order. Benedict would stand before them, not just as their leader, but as the embodiment of the Almighty's wrath. He would pronounce the tracker's crimes, his voice resonant with the power that thrummed within him. And then, with a mere gesture, he would unleash a fraction of the Almighty's might, a display of force that would leave no doubt about the consequences of defiance.

This act would serve a dual purpose. Not only would it quell any lingering thoughts of rebellion within the Order, but it would also send a clear message to the Crones. Their power, however formidable it may have seemed in the past, was nothing compared to the force that Benedict now wielded. The Almighty's will was absolute, and through Benedict, that will would be manifested.

The Crones, for all their supposed might, would soon learn the true extent of his power.

He raised his arms as the dark tendrils of magic swept out in a spectacle across the room, inciting a satisfying gasp from the gathered crowd before receding back into his being. "The Order of Crimson has been reborn, and in this new era, the Almighty's word is the whole of the law. The future is ours to shape," Benedict declared. "The Almighty's will be done, and through me, a new dawn shall rise. Let all who oppose us tremble, for their fate is sealed. The Order of Crimson shall be a beacon of perfection, a testament to the unyielding strength of the Almighty's chosen."

The members of the order knelt in reverence as Benedict's words washed over them like a dark tide.

He needed more. He needed to make an example out of someone, only the tracker was too far away. However, there was another traitor among them who deserved further punishment. He turned his attention back to the generals. “Where is the Cleric? The one who betrayed me?” he asked.

The generals looked at each other in puzzlement.

“Where is he? I demand that he step forward now, or be dragged here.”

“He was punished by the Elders,” Franklin, the senior General, spoke.

“It was not enough,” the Shepherd barked, and Franklin bowed his head in obedience. “Fine. If you will not fetch him, the power of the almighty will!”

He raised his arms again, letting the black tendrils fly out, seeking the traitor, to no avail.

“Where. Is. He!?” the Shepherd’s voice boomed.

“I saw him last in the garden, several days ago,” a monk in the front row spoke. “But not since then.”

The Cleric had defied him once, that was bad enough, but to escape the reach of the compound, that act deserved a far greater punishment. The Cleric would regret every step he’d taken to leave the compound. He would beg for mercy, and he’d suffer without the grace of death, because to live in pain and terror would be far worse. A black rage swam over Father Benedict and within that rage, his power bloomed.

34
INGRID

Ingrid sighed softly as she inhaled the scent of rosemary and sage. She had been tending to her herbs that morning, and when the last weed was pulled and thrown to the compost pile, she stood for a moment and surveyed her abode. In the dappled sunlight of late morning, Ingrid's hut with its thatched roof seemed almost to be a living part of the forest canopy.

Ingrid, attuned to the subtle shifts of her forest, sensed the approach of her fellow Crones. She walked towards her hut, just before Marjie, Agatha, and Delia appeared on the path through the trees. Delia's grandkids, bursts of youthful energy, dashed ahead, followed closely by Torin, the beagle puppy who the earth dragon so loved to emulate, his tail wagging in excitement.

"About time," Ingrid called out, her voice warm and inviting. "I'd assumed you'd taken a different mystical path and gotten lost in the forest or found a new coven to join."

Marjie responded with a chuckle. "Mystical path, indeed. There's no option but to take the scenic route all the way out here, Ingrid."

Agatha rolled her eyes. "My back aches from all this walking."

Delia grinned. "Scenic or not, there's always a sense of peace here."

"That's right, Nanna," said little Merryn gleefully. "It's like hopping into another world."

"Peaceful is another word for dull," Agatha grumbled.

Delia shook her head. "Peaceful, yes, but never dull. Especially not with that capricious dragon pup. Where is she hiding?"

No sooner had Delia spoken than the earth dragon emerged, huge and majestic, from around the side of the hut, her scales glinting in the sunlight. The grandkids gasped in delight, and Torin barked playfully. In an instant, the dragon transformed back into a playful puppy, much to Ingrid's frustration.

"See," said Keyne. "I told you she's a real dragon."

Merryn nodded. "But she likes to be a puppy."

"A dragon's whims are her own," Ingrid said with exasperation. "It seems she's as unpredictable as the wind. You should know all about that, Agatha."

"Enough about Agatha's wind," said Marjie with a cheeky grin. "Let's have some tea."

The Crones gathered around Ingrid's wooden table as the children played outside.

Marjie began sharing tales of her latest forays into potion-making. "I'm telling you, nettle extract is underrated. It's a bit of a sting to handle, but it works wonders."

Agatha leaned forward, her curiosity piqued. "Nettle extract sounds fine, but don't let the fresh leaves prick your bottom in the moonlight – you'll regret it."

"Now that sounds like a hilarious story," said Marjie. "Care to elaborate?"

"I'd rather she didn't," Ingrid said as she poured out cups of herbal tea, the steam carrying the scent of mint and chamomile.

Delia had been keeping an eye on the grandkids and Torin through the window but turned her attention back to the matters at hand. "Ingrid, any progress on your search in the swamp?"

Shaking her head, Ingrid replied, "It remains elusive, but the earth reveals its secrets in its own time. I'm not discouraged."

"Well, I'm just thrilled to have got my hands on my grimoire," said Marjie, her eyes twinkling in excitement as she reached into her bag, carefully pulling out the old, weathered book. Its cover, though worn, was etched with intricate patterns.

Ingrid leaned forward. "That's excellent, Marjie. I can only imagine the secrets it holds."

Agatha quirked an eyebrow. "Secrets, old gossip and family

recipes, no doubt. But Marjie, have you found any clues about the water dragon? Time isn't exactly on our side."

Marjie opened the grimoire, revealing pages filled with arcane symbols, cryptic notes, and recipes for potions and spells. "Not yet, but it's more than gossip and recipes, Agatha. There's knowledge here passed down through generations. Who knows what we might find that could help us in our quest?"

Ingrid's eyes traced the lines of text, pondering the possibilities. "Indeed. Family grimoires tend to contain more than meets the eye. The answers don't always reveal themselves straight away. Good things take time."

Agatha let out a huff. "Very well, but in the meantime, the world marches on and we still have no idea what we're doing!"

As the time came to depart, Delia made her way to Ingrid's back garden to gather the children, the other Crones following behind her.

The dragon, still in her playful puppy form, romped around with Merryn and Keyne, their laughter echoing through the air.

Ingrid, with a hint of jest in her voice, asked the children, "I don't suppose you kids have any clue where the earth dragon's relic might be?" She knew it was a long shot, but part of her held onto the hope that children, with their unburdened minds, might see what adults often overlooked.

Merryn, with the innocent earnestness of a child, reached out to pat the head of the dragon puppy. "Where's your relic? You good girl. Show me your relic," she implored in a sweet tone.

Ingrid rolled her eyes, amused by the child's simplicity. "If only it were that easy."

To everyone's surprise, the dragon puppy let out a loud belch, and something fell from its mouth, clattering to the ground.

The Crones and the children watched in astonishment as a glimmering stone rolled across the garden path. It was a beautiful deep green.

Ingrid's eyes widened in disbelief. She quickly stooped to pick up the stone, examining it closely. It was unmistakably the stone she'd been seeking – its energy resonated with the power of the earth.

"Of all the ways to find it," Ingrid muttered under her breath. She turned to the others, holding the stone up.

Marjie gasped. "Well, I'll be."

Agatha chuckled. "The earth dragon's stone, delivered in the most unorthodox manner."

Delia laughed. "Leave it to a dragon puppy to surprise us in the most unexpected ways."

Ingrid shook her head, a smile tugging at her lips. "The mysteries of the magical world never cease to amaze. And sometimes, it takes a child's request to unveil them."

Delia, with a sense of both amusement and awe, added, "It seems we underestimate both our familiars and the children. They have their own ways of uncovering magic."

Ingrid, holding the gleaming stone with a newfound reverence, looked at the dragon puppy, now frolicking with the children again. "Thank you, my friend," she said softly. The dragon, in her puppy form, wagged her tail, seemingly oblivious to the magnitude of her action.

35
MARJIE

Marjie sat in the comforting embrace of the crackling fire in her very own wing of Thorn Manor. She reached out to stroke the wooden panelling near her, appreciating the house and the way it had accommodated her so beautifully after having to leave her own home. The house purred beneath her hand like a satisfied cat.

Marjie smiled and took another sip of tea.

In her lap sat her family grimoire, its pages rich with the wit and wisdom of generations past. She set down her cup and opened the cover to delve once more into the depths of the book, searching for clues.

The fire's gentle warmth and the quiet of her surroundings created a perfect setting for reflection. Marjie's mind, however, was restless, her thoughts flitting from one spell to the next, one potion recipe to another, seeking connections and insights.

She'd been doing this for hours every day, staying up late

into the night, to no avail. Whatever the book was hiding, it was doing a bloody good job of it.

She'd carefully inspected each page, especially the blank ones which seemed to be positioned at random. Marjie spent rather a lot of time pondering whether these empty ones held secrets, or whether they were merely extra pages for new spells and recipes to be added.

She thumbed through the entire tome twice, then began again.

Only this time, as she turned a page, her hand brushed against her cup of tea sitting next to her. To her horror, the teacup tipped, spilling over the sacred pages of the grimoire.

"Oh blast!" she exclaimed, aghast at the potential damage to such a priceless family artifact. "Blast it all!"

She reached out to rectify the mishap, but before she could utter a charm to draw out the tea, something extraordinary happened.

A fine mist began to rise from the pages of the grimoire, shimmering in the firelight.

Marjie watched, spellbound, as the mist sparkled and twirled above the book, forming patterns of graceful beauty.

Then, as if guided by an unseen hand, silvery letters began to form across the page, writing themselves in an elegant script which glowed against a previously blank page.

Marjie's eyes widened in wonder and disbelief. The grimoire was revealing secrets of its own accord, secrets that had apparently been hidden from prying eyes, awaiting the right moment to be unveiled.

"Of course it was the tea," she muttered to herself. "Of course..."

She wanted to scold herself for not thinking of this sooner, yet, as the thought crossed her mind, so did the horror of pouring tea on an old book. Marjie snorted in laughter. "No, I would not have tried *that* any sooner," she chortled. "I suppose it's all happening in perfect time – exactly as it needs to unfold."

She leaned in closer as the letters continued to scrawl themselves along the page, forming words and sentences, weaving a message that seemed to Marjie to resonate with the very essence of magic itself.

Marjie leaned even closer, her heart racing with excitement and bursting with awe. This was no mere accident; it was a revelation, a gift from the grimoire itself.

Of course, the spilled tea had acted as a catalyst, unlocking ancient magic that had been dormant within the pages.

The room around her faded into insignificance as Marjie absorbed the wisdom unfolding before her. She felt a surge of gratitude and wonder. The grimoire, a relic of her family's magical heritage, had chosen this moment to reveal its deeper truths.

But, as Marjie continued to study the newly revealed script in her grimoire, her initial excitement gave way to a creeping sense of dismay. The words, cryptic yet unmistakably clear, suggested a journey that chilled her heart:

Beneath the waves, in depths untold,

Lies great power, magnificent and old.
Seek the heart where waters swirl,
In the silent deep, secrets unfurl.

Marjie's heart sank as she read and re-read the lines. The power she sought, the key to unlocking her potential, lay in the one place she had always feared the most: the deep, dark waters of the ocean. The very thought of venturing into such depths filled her with a cold dread that seemed to seep into her bones.

She had always had an uneasy relationship with water, particularly the vast, open sea. As a child, she'd had nightmares of its endless depths, of what lay beneath the surface, unseen and unknown. All this had haunted her since she was a child. And now, her path forward, the path to understanding her own power, required her to face this fear head-on.

Marjie sat back, the grimoire resting heavily in her lap. The fire's warmth did little to dispel the chill that had settled over her. She knew that her fellow Crones, Ingrid, Agatha, and Delia, would offer their support, but this was a journey *she* would have to undertake, with or without them.

The sea, with its hidden depths and secrets, called to her, and she could not ignore its call.

She continued to read.

In the ocean's embrace, you'll find your fate,
Where waters deep do not abate.

Embrace the fear, dive into the oblivious night,
In the sea's heart lies your true valour and might.

Marjie took a deep, steadying breath, her mind racing. The journey ahead would not be easy, but she knew it was necessary. To unlock the full extent of her water powers, to fulfil her destiny as a Crone of Myrtlewood, she would have to confront her deepest fear.

With determination and deep dread, Marjie closed the grimoire. The path ahead was clear, though daunting. She would prepare herself, both mentally and magically, for what lay beneath the waves. The deep waters called to her, and she would answer, for the sake of the mysteries that bound them all.

36
THE CLERIC

The Cleric felt a churning quagmire of emotions as he continued on his journey through the countryside, having renounced his vows and turned his back on the sacred brethren that had defined his entire life. He was no longer the Cleric of the Order of Crimson, yet his given name, Cedric, seemed foreign to him. Perhaps he could retain his own title, now a Cleric of a far more important role.

The decision to leave had not been easy; but it was ultimately his only option. He could not sit idly by and therefore he must risk everything and step into an unknown world, one that he had been taught to view with suspicion and disdain.

Beneath the blazing midday sun, the Cleric's resolve burned hotter than ever as he strode out of the forest and through the fields, eyes fixed on his target: a lone horse grazing in the distance. The animal stood apart from the others, its frame lean and weary, bearing the scars of neglect.

Its coat was matted and unkempt, reflecting the hardships it had endured. Yet, despite its condition, there was a glimmer of strength in its gaze, a resilience that spoke of survival against the odds.

With each step closed, his heart pounded with urgency. He needed to move swiftly, before the Order came after him. He did not know how long it would take them to notice his absence. Under his old role, his departure would have been recognised immediately; however, having lost all standing within the Order and reduced to the lowest ranks, his existence warranted little attention and for this small mercy he was grateful. However, at some point they would notice, and given his recent betrayal of the Crimson Shepherd, he wouldn’t be surprised if it was sooner rather than later that his former mentor sought further penitence.

For now, he had to focus. He needed a steed to carry him as far away as possible from the life he'd left behind.

Closing the distance, he moved swiftly, his movements fluid and purposeful. Without hesitation, he approached the horse, his hands moving with practiced ease as he swiftly untethered it from its post.

The horse whinnied softly, its eyes reflecting. The Cleric swung himself onto its back. Despite its outward appearance of fragility, the animal remained steady beneath him.

The Cleric couldn't help but feel a pang of sympathy for the creature, a small solace in knowing that he had liberated it from a life of neglect, even if only to serve as his mount on his quest.

With a swift kick of his heels, they were off, the wind whipping through the Cleric's hair as they thundered across the fields. Behind them, the farmstead faded into the distance like a vague dream upon waking.

In this manner, he made his way towards the village of Myrtlewood.

This quaint town, often whispered about within the Order as a source of trouble and unorthodox magic, was now his destination. It was here that he believed he would find the root of the chaos, the source of the disturbance that he was compelled to destroy.

As he rode, the Cleric's thoughts were a blur. He was no longer bound by the rigid codes and dogmas; he was his own man, free to act as he saw fit. Yet, this freedom came with a weight of responsibility and uncertainty.

The journey took him through countryside that gradually shifted from the familiar rugged terrain of the mountains to the more gentle landscapes that surrounded the village. The closer he got, the more he observed the simple beauty of the world outside the Order – the fields teeming with life, the woods alive with the sounds of nature, the streams flowing with clear water.

But beneath this serene facade, the Cleric felt a growing sense of unease. Myrtlewood was not just another village; it was a place of hidden powers and secrets, a place that the Order had viewed with suspicion for good reason. He knew that the inhabitants of Myrtlewood might not take kindly to a former member of the Order, especially one with his intentions.

As he approached the outskirts of Myrtlewood, the Cleric

slowed his pace. The village lay ahead, its cottages and buildings nestled among the trees, illuminated in the golden light of the near-setting sun.

With a deep breath, the Cleric steeled himself for what was to come. His old life was behind him. Now, he was an agent of his own destiny, a man on a mission that he believed was just and necessary.

The Cleric had arrived at his destination.

The public house known as the Witch's Wort was a quaint establishment. He allowed himself to absorb its charming ambiance.

The walls seemed to be adorned with old paintings and relics of bygone times. The wooden beams overhead were aged and sturdy, bearing witness to countless tales and secrets whispered under their watch. The air was filled with the aroma of hearty stew and the sweet scent of freshly baked bread.

The patrons of the Witch's Wort were likely village locals and travellers, their voices blending into a harmonious murmur of laughter and conversation. A bard strummed a lute in the corner, adding a melodic undertone to the din.

Despite the warm atmosphere, the Cleric couldn't shake off his ingrained prejudices and discomfort.

The presence of women in the public house, mingling freely and openly, was a stark contrast to the doctrines of the Order where they were seen as the enemy.

The Cleric found his stomach churning. His experience with women was almost non-existent. He felt a wave of mild nausea at the prospect of engaging with them, yet he knew he couldn't waver. His mission was clear, and he needed to muster the courage to see it through.

As he moved through the large busy room, his steps measured and cautious, he tempered the conflict within himself. The laughter and light around him were so at odds with the sombre, rigid world he had come from.

He found a secluded spot at the back of the room, his eyes scanning around, taking in the faces of patrons.

He sat alone, torn between the world he had known and the reality that confronted him.

The woman from the bar approached with a confident stride and a friendly smile.

"Hello there. I'm Sherry. I don't think we've met."

He nodded, curtly.

She paused, as if assessing him. The Cleric froze, unsure of the proper way to engage in conversation with a woman.

“And you are?” she asked, with a trace of suspicion.

"Cedric," the Cleric muttered, his voice barely above a whisper. The name felt alien to him, so rarely had he used his own name, always known by his title within the Order. He couldn't help but think of the irony in Sherry's name, given her profession.

"Sherry," Cedric muttered. “Isn't that a confusing name for a tavern wench?”

Sherry laughed, a sound as rich and warm as the tavern itself. "Like I haven't heard that one before! And besides, I'm hardly a wench – you cheeky beggar. I own the place."

Cedric averted his gaze, momentarily caught in the grip of old prejudices. Women owning businesses? The thought was abhorrent to the Order and all it stood for, but he knew better than to voice such opinions.

Sherry laughed, and the sound surprised him, ringing warmly like a bell.

"What brings you to the Witch's Wort, Cedric?" Sherry asked with curiosity.

Cedric raised his head, meeting her gaze. The feeling of loss, of being unmoored from the Order, hit him again. "Just passing through," he said, his voice steadier than he felt.

"You look like you could do with some cheering up. How about a mulled mead and a bowl of hearty stew?" Sherry suggested.

He nodded, not fully trusting his voice. Sherry's warmth was disarming, and despite his reservations, he found himself returning her smile, albeit hesitantly.

As she turned to fetch his order, Cedric sat back, taking in the lively atmosphere surrounding him, so different from the cold, austere halls of the Order.

In that moment, amidst the lively bustle of the Witch's Wort, Cedric felt a stirring of something long suppressed – a sense of connection, of being part of a world much larger and more varied than the one he had known. It was both unsettling and strangely liberating.

37
DELIA

Delia was enjoying a quiet lunch with Kitty, bathing in the warmth of winter sunlight shining in through the window. The aroma of buttered toast and coffee filled the air. The grandchildren had been picked up the previous evening by Gilly, who'd seemed to be in a rush and didn't have time to chat, sparking more anxiety within Delia, but she was trying not to think about that, just as she was trying not to think about how little progress she'd made in getting access to her family grimoire. Every time she thought about contacting Elamina, something held her back. Ruminating on all this was doing her no good at all.

"Why are you looking glum?" Kitty asked. "Is it the absence of your handsome rogue?"

Delia sighed. "No, it's probably guilt that I'm not doing more to get my hands on that blasted grimoire. I was so focussed on making sure you were okay."

“No one asked you to do that,” Kitty grumbled.

“Well, you wouldn’t ask for help, would you?” Delia nudged Kitty with her elbow. “Anyway, I haven’t made any progress.”

“Wouldn’t the next logical step be to ask Elamina for help?” Kitty asked. “She’s your cousin and she seemed to care about you enough to help rescue you.”

“Yes, but every time I think of it, I wonder whether I’ve already asked too much, and then I have other doubts – like what if Elamina has her own agenda? I’m not totally sure I can trust her and my instinct tells me to hold my cards close to my chest.”

“Well, who am I to argue with your instinct?” Kitty rolled her eyes. “Anyway, what are we doing today?”

As they were chatting about the day's plans, there was an unexpected knock at the door. Delia rose to answer it to find Marjie, looking notably flustered.

"Come in, come in!" Delia ushered her friend into the cottage.

Kitty, ever the gracious host, quickly set about making a pot of tea, sensing that Marjie needed a bit of comfort.

Once settled at the kitchen table with a steaming cup of tea in front of her, Marjie began to explain. "I was going through my family grimoire, and I accidentally spilled tea on it.”

"Oh no!" Delia cried, picturing the ancient pages ruined by a careless spill. The grimoire was a treasure trove of knowledge and magic, and the thought of it being damaged was beyond distressing.

Marjie shook her head, her expression turning more serious. "That's not the problem, dear. The grimoire is fine." She paused, taking a deep breath.

"Oh," said Delia, taken aback. "Then what is it?"

"It's what happened after," Marjie continued. "The spill...it revealed something in the book."

"But that's wonderful!" said Delia, squinting in confusion. "Isn't it? You were looking for clues for days...but your face says it isn't wonderful at all."

Marjie sighed deeply. "The book tells me, in no uncertain terms, that an underwater journey is required to fully harness my powers."

Delia's eyes widened in understanding. "The water dragon..." she murmured, piecing the information together. It made sense, in a way. It seemed the elements and their corresponding creatures were often linked in deep, mystical ways.

Delia shuddered slightly. *Does that mean I'm going to have to walk through fire?*

She shook her head to dislodge the alarming thought and focused back on Marjie.

"So...you need to go into the sea?" Delia said, lightly. "Like... going for a swim?"

Marjie nodded. "Yes, but I'm deathly afraid of the ocean!" Her voice trembled as she spoke.

Delia reached across the table, offering a comforting hand. "Oh, Marjie, we'll figure this out. You're not alone in this."

She could empathise with Marjie's fear. After all, the ocean was vast with its mysterious depths.

They sat in the warm kitchen, sipping their tea. Delia could see the turmoil in Marjie's eyes – the conflict between wanting to fulfil her duty as a Crone and her deep-seated fear of the sea. It was a daunting prospect, to face one's deepest fears head-on.

Delia pondered over the problem, her brows knitting together in thought. "There must be some way to journey under water safely. Maybe a submarine?"

Kitty, who had been quietly listening, couldn't help but roll her eyes at the suggestion. "Where are you going to get one of those!"

Marjie, however, smiled, a glint of mischief in her eyes. "If only it were that simple. Rosemary knows exactly where we could borrow one of those, but I get the impression we need to be *in* the water, not just in a craft of some sort."

Delia leaned back in her chair. "What about magic? Surely there's magic that can help us to breathe underwater."

"I've no doubt there is," Marjie replied, her smile fading slightly. "But where would we even start? Perhaps we could just skip this part and hope the water dragon eventually finds us? We have no one to guide us into the murky depths, and besides, the thought of going out into the deep ocean, even using magic, still sounds abjectly terrifying to me!"

“I'm afraid you won't be able to just skip this step,” said Kitty.

“Why not?” Marjie asked woefully.

“Because, I'm the sort of person who always tries to skip the important steps and always ends up in more trouble. You think I'd have learnt by now.” Kitty batted her eyelids.

“Indeed,” said Delia, with a playful smile. “And why haven't you learnt your lesson?”

“So I can be an example to others, clearly.” Kitty smirked. “I’m self-sacrificing like that.”

Marjie sighed deeply. “I’m afraid you’re right, at any rate. There is no way to wriggle out of this one, though I desperately want to. I suppose it’s all that face-your-fears nonsense. It is humbling, at any rate. The Water Crone afraid of her own element! Some powerful witch I’ve turned out to be! I might as well be afraid of my own shadow like a cowardly cat.”

“Don’t be so hard on yourself,” said Kitty. “Most people never face their fears and spend the vast majority of their lives running from them.”

“Kitty’s right,” said Delia. “You’re no coward. You’re one of the strongest, bravest people I know. Your fears are understandable, and they don’t make you a lesser person. Not in the least.”

“Perhaps you’re right,” said Marjie, her tea cup trembling slightly in her hand. “But I still have no idea how to proceed.”

"We'll find a way, Marjie," Delia said, reassuringly patting her friend’s hand. "We’ll start by researching any spells or enchantments that might help. There’s bound to be something in one of our grimoires or the many books Agatha has."

Kitty nodded. "Surely, someone in Myrtlewood knows this stuff," she said. "Vampires and werewolves are real, after all. What about mermaids? Don’t you have any of them?"

Marjie's face broke into a smile, the tension easing slightly. "We have a merman, actually," she revealed, "but he’s never around in the winters."

"Merman?" Kitty raised an eyebrow, her curiosity piqued.

"Is he as hot as a certain Hollywood depiction that springs to mind?"

Marjie cackled and playfully batted at Kitty's hand. "Oh, you! He's not bad looking, I'll give you that, but that's hardly relevant, especially as he's not here to help us right now."

Delia pondered this new piece of information. "It seems we know all the right ingredients," she mused, "we just need to figure out how to acquire them and what order to put them into the cauldron..."

Marjie smiled at Delia's words. "Talking like a true witch," she said, the corners of her mouth rising into a small smile. "You're right. We need a recipe, and I know all about recipes."

Delia beamed at her. "Indeed you do! We'll need to do some research. And maybe seek advice from others."

Kitty nodded. "And I suppose we'll need to prepare ourselves, both magically and mentally. If a merman can live underwater, surely there's a way for Marjie to safely accomplish her aquatic escapade."

"Actually," Marjie said, her mind working rapidly, "Mervyn does have a few close friends around Myrtlewood, and I do profess to know everyone in town. Maybe there's a way to get hold of him."

"Mervyn the Merman!" Kitty crowed. "This place is unbelievable."

"Quiet, you," Delia playfully scolded, though a smile tugged at her lips. The absurdity of their situation wasn't lost on her, but in Myrtlewood, the absurd often became the norm in many ways. Delia shook her head and turned her attention back to Marjie who rubbed her chin thoughtfully. The prospect of reaching out to Mervyn the merman offered a glimmer of hope in their quest.

Kitty leaned back in her chair, her expression turning mischievous. "It sounds to me like you're in for another adventure," she said. "I'd best be invited this time."

Delia frowned, her concern for Kitty evident. "After the whole portal fiasco? You're joking. I was scared we'd lost you."

"Don't be silly," Kitty retorted with a dismissive wave of her hand. "It would take more than a pesky portal to keep me down."

Marjie, who had been listening intently, took a big gulp of her tea. "You know, I have a few ideas as to who to ask about Mervyn. We might be able to get in touch with him and find out what he has to say on the matter." She paused, a knowing look in her eye. "He seems to get along well with my good friend Papa Jack, so I'll start there."

Delia's smile broadened. The friendship between Marjie and Papa Jack was well-known in Myrtlewood, and she'd speculated there might be a deeper connection between them.

As they finished their tea, the morning's worries gave way to a renewed sense of purpose. "Oh, thank you for the support," Marjie said, giving Delia's hand a squeeze. "My journey to the depths might be fraught with fear, but the support of my friends gives me hope, at least."

"Hope is important," said Delia. "And we'll be here for you, no matter how scary things get."

38
MARJIE

Marjie stepped into the familiar scent of rich chocolate and sweet spices. Rosemary's charming shop was a haven of delectable magic, a place where fine ingredients became extraordinary marvels.

As she walked in, the bell above the door chimed, announcing her arrival. Papa Jack, who was here even more than Rosemary was these days, looked up from behind the counter, a smile spreading across his face. Marjie smiled back at him. Her good friend was always the epitome of a dapper gentleman with his neatly trimmed beard and clean pressed shirt under his lavender-and-mint striped apron.

"Marjie, my dear, what brings you here today?" he asked, his voice rich and welcoming.

"I was hoping to catch you for a little chat, maybe get some advice," Marjie replied, her eyes wandering over the array of chocolates on display.

"Of course, but first, you must try some of Rosemary's new truffles. She's been experimenting."

He held up a plate of assorted truffles.

"That sounds marvellous. Ooh, what are these ones?" She picked up a truffle that seemed to swirl with dark blues and greens.

"Ahh, you chose well," he replied as she bit into the treat. "I call that one the siren's song. It's soothing and delicious with oceanic flavours!"

Marjie felt her eyes widen as the flavour of salted caramel mixed with a hint of pepper and seaweed exploded on her tongue, a surprising combination that somehow worked perfectly. A sense of calm washed over her.

"You know, if you'd told me it represented the ocean before I'd picked it up, I'd probably have chosen differently, but that was actually rather lovely. I'd better have another one."

"Try this." Papa Jack gestured towards a truffle that looked to be dusted with a fine, golden powder. It tasted of honey and chamomile, a relaxing and comforting blend. As the flavour melted on her palate, Marjie felt a warmth spread through her, a gentle happiness that made her smile.

As Marjie savoured the flavours of Rosemary's magical truffles, Papa Jack leaned against the counter. "You know, Marjie, you always seem to find yourself in the heart of the storm. You're braver than most."

Marjie chuckled, a blush creeping into her cheeks. "I wouldn't say brave, more like 'accidentally adventurous'." Marjie felt a small swell of guilt. There was so much she hadn't told him, but perhaps now she could finally explain everything that had happened over the winter.

Papa Jack raised an eyebrow, a playful smirk on his lips. "Accidentally adventurous? Is that what we're calling it these days? Next, you'll be telling me you 'accidentally' became one of the most powerful witches in Myrtlewood."

Marjie narrowed her eyes at him. “Maybe I have.”

“I wouldn’t doubt that, not even for a second.”

She popped another truffle into her mouth, aware that she was stalling. But how could she explain so much? She searched her mind for the right words. This one burst with the flavour of spiced orange and cinnamon, leaving a tingling sensation on her tongue and a burst of energy that lifted her spirits. “Oh, that one is divine!”

Papa Jack watched her with a pleased expression. "Rosemary has outdone herself, hasn't she?”

Marjie nodded, savouring the lingering taste. "They're incredible, as always.”

“Now, tell me, why was it you’d have rejected the oceanic truffle?”

Marjie lowered her gaze. “I’m afraid there’s rather a lot I haven’t told you and it’s a long story.” She began to explain the secrets she’d been holding back about the Myrtlewood Crones, bracing herself for a reaction, but Papa Jack merely listened quietly with compassion in his eyes.

“I knew there was something you were holding back from me, my dear,” he said.

“I’m so sorry I couldn’t tell you about all this before,” said Marjie. “I really wanted to, but Agatha swore me to secrecy. I suppose it was necessary at first. I mean, we didn't even know if we were the fabled crones and we didn't understand the risks involved. Now, it appears the cat is out of the bag and you're the first person I wanted to tell, after Rosemary and Athena."

"I'm glad you've finally told me," Papa Jack said. "But what does this have to do with the ocean?"

"I said it was a long story..." Marjie explained about finally finding her family grimoire, tears springing up in her eyes as she spoke of her brother, Graham, and how he had only been avoiding her in order to protect her.

Papa Jack came out from behind the counter and wrapped Marjie in a big hug, comforting her as she continued the story, including the tea incident with the grimoire and her deep-seated fears about the underwater journey it spoke of. It was cathartic – letting everything out like this – and Papa Jack was always an excellent listener. It soothed Marjie's soul to tell him everything now, bridging the gap that had begun to form between them – the gap created by Marjie's secrets and fears.

"So, you see, I need more information – I need to find someone who understands the underwater realm."

"And you thought of Mervyn?" Papa Jack said.

Marjie nodded. "Only, I have no idea how to get in touch with him. He's never here in the winter as you know. I wondered if he'd told you anything, seeing as you two love playing croquet together on Sundays – or at least you did before he left as the frosts rolled in."

Papa Jack listened intently, his eyes thoughtful.

"I might know a way to reach Mervyn," he said after a moment.

Marjie felt a surge of relief and gratitude. Coming to Papa Jack had been the right decision. Not only had she found comfort in Rosemary's magical truffles, she had also found a glimmer of hope.

As she left Myrtlewood Chocolates, a small box of truffles in hand, Marjie felt a renewed sense of determination and a warmth that spread her smile from ear to ear, despite her fears.

39
AGATHA

The icy morning had draped Agatha's farmhouse in a frosty blanket. Agatha stood in the backyard, her breath forming little puffs of steam in the cold air. Her eyes were fixed on the small, intricate pendant in her hand – the one tangible connection to the air dragon she possessed.

Agatha tried, yet again, to coax the air dragon out of its pendant form. The pendant, however, remained stubbornly unresponsive, much to her growing frustration.

"Come on, you stubborn thing," Agatha muttered under her breath. "It's not like I'm asking you to move mountains. I just want to have a chat."

She tried various incantations, each one spoken with a blend of respect and impatience. The pendant, however, was indifferent to her efforts. It lay cold and still in her palm.

Agatha sighed, her breath misting in the frigid air. "You're as uncooperative as a cat on a rainy day," she grumbled, shaking the pendant slightly as if to wake it from slumber.

A sudden gust of wind swept over her. Agatha narrowed her eyes. "Was that you?" she whispered to the pendant.

More gusts of wind followed, swirling around her in brief, intense bursts. The winds whipped her hair and cloak, sending loose leaves and small twigs dancing in mini cyclones around her.

"Whoa there!" Agatha exclaimed, steadying herself against the unexpected gusts. "I asked for a dragon, not a tempest!"

The pendant pulsed in her hand, as if it were alive. Agatha continued her entreaties, her coaxing and exasperation.

"Come on, now. Don't be shy. I know you're in there," she coaxed, then added with a hint of annoyance, "You're as fickle as the wind itself."

Agatha, not one to be easily deterred, continued her efforts. Her words became more rhythmic, almost melodic, as she harmonised her incantations with the natural energy around her. The icy air of the morning stilled as if to wait in anticipation.

Suddenly, without warning, the pendant glowed with a fierce light, and in a rush of power, the air dragon manifested before her. Majestic and powerful, it unfurled its ethereal wings, sending a gale-force wind swirling around the surrounding farmland.

Agatha braced herself as her hair and cloak whipped wildly about as she took in the awe-inspiring sight of the air dragon. A creature of sheer elemental force hovered before her, its eyes gleaming with an intelligence that transcended words. Leaves and small debris from the yard were caught up in the vortex, dancing chaotically in the air around the creature.

For a moment, Agatha was stunned as she took in the full majesty and power of the dragon. Despite seeing the creature before, the sight was still a shock to the senses.

Then, a thrill of excitement surged through her as she made her mental calculations. "I can work with this!"

The challenge of interacting with such a powerful creature was exhilarating.

The air dragon, with its immense presence, seemed to acknowledge her spirit, its gusts softening slightly as if in response to her enthusiasm.

As the wind whipped around her, a distant voice cut through the howling wind, calling her name. "Agatha!" it shouted, persistent and concerned.

The air dragon dissolved back into the pendant, the gusts of wind dying down as swiftly as they had arisen.

“Oh bother,” Agatha muttered.

Covvey, her old friend, came ambling over through the settling leaves and twigs. His weathered face showed concern and curiosity as he approached her.

"Are you okay there, Agatha?" he asked, his eyes scanning her for any sign of distress.

Agatha straightened up, brushing her hands over her wildly tousled white hair in an attempt to tame it.

With a gleam in her eye, she replied, "I'm spiffing, Covvey. I think I'm finally getting somewhere with all this crone and dragon nonsense." Her voice carried a tone of triumph and a hint of exhilaration from her recent encounter.

“Glad to hear it,” he replied gruffly.

"Why are you here, Covvey?" Agatha asked.

Covvey shrugged, his hands in his pockets. "I just came to check on you.”

Agatha frowned slightly in mild annoyance. "What are you checking up on me for?"

Covvey frowned. "Not a crime, is it?"

Agatha sighed. "Well, I suppose it's good to know someone's looking out for me. Now, it’s rather chilly out here, would you care to come in for a sherry by the fire?"

Covvey grimaced. “You know I don’t care for that sweet drivel. Offer me some whiskey and I’ll be there in a flash.”

40
MARJIE

The salty tang of the sea air mixed with the earthy scent of the nearby forest as Marjie and Papa Jack strolled down towards the beach. The wintery shore was deserted, with only the cries of the gulls and the crash and whisper of the waves breaking and rolling.

"We need to find one," Marjie said. "Not just bring one from home?"

"That's right," Papa Jack replied. "That's what Mervyn told me."

They walked along, close to the water's edge, their feet sinking into the damp sand, scanning the beach for the perfect object.

Finally, Marjie spotted one, half-buried near a tuft of sea grass. "There!" She pointed.

"You're right," Papa Jack said as Marjie unearthed it. "The perfect shell."

It was a beautiful conch, its spiral smooth and the colour of sun-bleached bone.

"How did something so gorgeous wash up here? Surely this must be from tropical waters," Marjie muttered.

"The ocean is vast and mysterious."

Marjie sighed. "Don't remind me. Are you sure this will work?" She held the shell up to the light, its pinkish interior gleaming.

Papa Jack shrugged, his eyes crinkling with a smile. "Not sure," he replied. "But, like I said, I did happen to ask Mervyn over my regular plum sorbet how one would contact him in the off-season. He laughed and told me he didn't do ice-cream runs in the winter, but that if anyone really needed to get in touch, this is how they'd do it. He called it his shell-phone."

Marjie chuckled, shaking her head. "Oh, Mervyn. I suppose it's better reception than we get with the mobiles out here."

Papa Jack joined in her laughter. "Indeed. And much more environmentally friendly, I might add."

They carefully placed a message inside the shell – a simple note written on a slip of parchment that Marjie had prepared earlier. Marjie then sealed it with a charm, her fingers tracing symbols that glowed momentarily upon the shell's surface.

Marjie took a deep breath, picturing Mervyn in her mind – a vivid image of the merman with his iridescent scales and playful eyes. She began to chant, her voice carrying over the waves, each word a ripple that stretched out into the vastness of the ocean.

. . .

Whispers of the ocean deep,
Heed our promises to keep,
As we will, magic's release,
Grant us passage, seas of peace.

Moments later she threw the shell into the frothy waves. It was immediately swallowed by the sea, hopefully taken by the currents to wherever Mervyn might be. They both watched the spot where the shell had disappeared, hopeful yet uncertain.

Afterwards, they settled down on the pebbly shore, spreading out a blanket against the cold. They unpacked a winter picnic, with thermoses filled with tea, and hot sandwiches wrapped in wax paper.

"So, what's the plan if Mervyn does show up?" Papa Jack asked, handing her a steaming cup of tea.

Marjie wrapped her hands around the cup, savouring the warmth. "Well, I suppose we ask him about his underwater world. How to navigate it, how to survive it...And maybe find out if he has any clue as to where we need to get to."

Papa Jack nodded. "And if he doesn't show up?"

Marjie gave him a wry smile. "Then we keep trying. We're witches, after all. Stubbornness is part of the job description."

They laughed and continued their meal, enjoying the quiet companionship and the beauty of the winter beach. The sky was a sprawl of greys and blues, and the sea was a shifting mirror, reflecting the changing moods above.

As they ate, they talked of past adventures and future plans, the laughter and the shared memories a warm counterpoint to the cold beach around them. And all the while, they kept an eye on the ocean, waiting for a sign from Mervyn.

Marjie shivered. Two hours had passed, with the sun now hanging low in the sky casting long shadows on the beach.

Marjie and Papa Jack were engrossed in conversation about Myrtlewood's many mysteries, when a gentle chime interrupted them, a sound like a crystal bell resonating with the ocean's breath.

A glow appeared on the horizon, a single point of light bobbing on the water's surface, growing brighter against the dimming sky. It moved with purpose towards the shore, weaving through the waves with grace.

As the light approached, it took on the hue of moonstone, then vanished.

"What was that?" Marjie asked. "Do you think it was something to do with us?"

"I can only hope it was," said Papa Jack. "Look!"

A shell, imbued with the same luminescence, washed up onto the shore nearby.

Marjie scrambled to retrieve it.

"Look, there's a note," said Papa Jack, pointing inside the shell.

Indeed, the note inside was unmistakably from Mervyn, the script flowing like the water he called home, and it confirmed their hopes: he would aid them in their quest.

"The muirgheilt potion," Marjie read aloud, feeling the

hairs stand up on the back of her neck. "He says we'll need it to see our quest through."

Papa Jack leaned over to take a look at the note. "Muirgheilt..."

Marjie shook her head. “I’ve heard of it...the sea's enchantment. It must be rather rare. It's been years since I've heard mention of such a potion. I don’t even know what it does!"

“I suppose you’ll find out,” Papa Jack said with a reassuring grin. “What else does it say?”

"In three days’ time," she mused. "Here, where the land meets the sea, we'll begin our true journey."

Marjie looked back towards the sea, where the light had been.

Papa Jack nodded. “Then let’s get back to town and find out more about this potion.”

They both stood up, packing away the remnants of their picnic. Marjie smiled at her good friend, happy to lend a hand and go above and beyond. She sighed gently, the world around them quiet except for the sound of the waves whispering to the shore.

41
DELIA

Delia approached Thorn Manor, a sense of trepidation filling her as she walked towards the grand home with its solitary vine-covered tower.

The door opened to reveal a slightly dishevelled woman with long wavy red hair.

"Delia. How wonderful to see you," Rosemary said, giving her a quick hug. "It seems like ages since the portal incident. How are you holding up? How's Kitty? Gosh, was that really only last week...?"

Rosemary continued in this vein and Delia smiled, bemused. When there was finally a pause, she explained that she and Kitty were both fine.

Rosemary sighed. "Oh good," she said. "Excuse the rambling. I do it when I'm nervous." She lowered her voice. "I'm worried about Marjie. I hope you Crones haven't gotten yourself in too deep."

Delia's smile turned from bemused to sympathetic. "It seems we've been thrown into this situation," she said. "I'm not sure there's much we can do other than follow our paths and do our best."

Rosemary nodded. "I can understand that, having had a similar experience of Myrtlewood, myself. Oh, what am I doing, making you stand out here in the cold! Come in."

As she entered, the warmth was a sharp contrast to the chill outside.

Rosemary led her to the kitchen, offering her a cup of tea. Athena sat at the table, but stood to greet Delia as she entered, offering a bright smile.

Moments later, Agatha and Ingrid made their entrance. Ingrid, wrapped in a cloak still carrying the scent of pine and earth from her forest home, grumbled softly, "I swear, if it weren't for you lot, I'd never leave my trees."

Agatha shook her head. "And miss all the fun? I think you enjoy our little escapades more than you let on."

"Ah, there you all are," Marjie said, entering the kitchen with a slightly frantic expression. "Now let's get started. Follow me."

As they all settled into the plush chairs of Thorn Manor's drawing room, Marjie began to unravel the tale of her grimoire's message and the unexpected communication with Mervyn.

Agatha listened with a sceptical raise of her eyebrow, her arms crossed as she absorbed the story. "You must be barking mad," she finally said. "You want us to go into the sea? What are we, Crones or water-babies?"

Ingrid leaned forward. "Water folk...I've always wondered about them."

Athena smiled. "It sounds thrilling, really."

Rosemary rolled her eyes. "Really?"

Delia looked around the room in growing discomfort. "I know you said underwater," she said slowly, the reality of the situation dawning on her. "You told me about that the last time we spoke...but I suppose it's only just now sinking in. I can understand why it terrifies you, Marjie. I don't understand how it's even possible."

Marjie nodded solemnly. "Neither did I, and I can guarantee you I'm more frightened than the lot of you put together. But I'm getting my head around it all. I'm hoping that with Mervyn's help, we might just find a way. And the muirgheilt potion could be the key."

"It's just...a bit much," said Delia.

Rosemary patted Delia's shoulder, her touch gentle and reassuring. "I know the feeling," she said with a soft smile. "A year ago, I knew nothing of magic, and now it's the air I breathe. You're doing fabulously."

Delia managed a small, grateful smile at Rosemary's encouragement, but her mind was still full of concerns. "But how will we...breathe?"

"That's where the potion comes in," Marjie said. "I've been doing a bit of research, with Athena's help. The muirgheilt potion apparently allows land-dwelling creatures like us to breathe underwater."

Agatha shook her head. "That's a rare potion. In all my years, I've never encountered it. I've only ever heard rumours.

Now you want to stake our lives on it?" Her voice was thick with disbelief and a hint of admiration for the boldness of the plan.

Delia smiled at her reassuringly, though she felt far from self-assured.

Ingrid's expression was exactly that of an excited child. "What an adventure!" she crowed, her eyes sparkling. "To think we could explore a whole new world – traverse the realm of water like the creatures who call it home!"

Delia's confusion remained. "What exactly does the potion do?"

"Oh, you'll see," said Marjie, her enthusiasm bubbling over like a potion in a cauldron. "It's something quite special."

“And how do we even make it?” Agatha asked.

Athena, who had been rifling through her own collection of magical texts, held up an old book with a triumphant flourish. "I've found a recipe here," she announced.

Marjie grinned as she pored over the recipe. "That's just like the one in my family grimoire, which is not only promising, it means that my ancestors have done this before!"

Agatha scowled at the list of ingredients, her experienced eyes quickly taking in the challenge they presented. “Seaweed is easy enough to find,” she muttered, her finger tracing down the page, “but seahorse pearls are rare, and abyssal coral dust? I've never even heard of it! Plus, we need at least three drops of bioluminescent algae oil and a sprig of enchanted kelp. And that's before we even consider the binding agents. This could take months...”

"We don't have months," Marjie said, her brow furrowing. "Mervyn is coming back to help us in three days!"

Delia felt a weight settle in her stomach. "How are we going to get all of those in three days?"

Rosemary gave her a knowing look. "We don't have them here," she admitted, "but I know someone who'd be able to find them, and it turns out we're both related to her."

Delia's mind raced. "Elamina," she said. "I don't know...I've been meaning to ask her about our family grimoire but I've been holding off on that, especially after she already went out of her way to help rescue me."

"You don't completely trust her, do you?" said Rosemary.

"I hardly know her," said Delia. "But I suppose not. There's something very odd about that whole family."

Rosemary nodded vigorously.

Delia frowned. "I'm worried if I keep running to her for help she won't want anything to do with me and I'll get further away from that grimoire."

"Or perhaps she'll just get used to helping you, and want to do it again," Marjie said. "Besides, you never asked her for help with the rescue. She came to you. That's a good sign."

Delia turned to Rosemary. "Do you think Elamina would want to help with the ingredients?"

Rosemary shrugged. "She helped me out once, with something similar. And she doesn't even like me." Her smile broadened into a grin. "I suspect she's rather fonder of you, considering she went to the effort to help save you from the Sisterhood."

Delia rubbed her eyes, feeling slightly overwhelmed. She didn't trust the Bracewells, but she had rather warmed to Elamina.

Delia let out a long slow breath. "I suppose all I can do is ask."

42
ELAMINA

Elamina sat in her office, the walls adorned with magical relics and other powerful symbols of her political stature within the witching parliament of Bermuda. The room was a monument of her ambition and success, filled with artifacts and tomes of power and influence. Her desk was meticulously organised with papers and parchments all in line. She frowned as she read the latest briefing from the Arch Magistrate's office. Pixies running amok? Really? Surely there were more important things to deal with.

Her focus was interrupted by the familiar chime of her communication crystal. She glanced at it, her expression shifting from concentration to curiosity as she recognised the signature. It wasn't from a magical source at all, it was from a mundane mechanical device – someone was calling her.

"Delia? This is a surprise," Elamina said, not impolitely.

"Uh, hello, Elamina." Delia's voice came through, clear despite the distance, her face swimming into view. Mundane technology had certainly improved in the past few decades – now it was almost as good as magical communication had been for centuries. "I'm sorry to bother you," Delia continued. "But I need a favour."

Elamina suppressed an eyeroll. Of course she was only called on to be useful. But, despite the request, she was intrigued. "What is it you need?" she asked in a non-committal voice.

Delia smiled at her, hopeful. "I need some potion ingredients. Can you help?"

Elamina raised an eyebrow. A request for potion ingredients wasn't totally surprising. The Bracewells were known for having some rather rare items in stock. She momentarily wondered what the Crones were up to. Surely Aunt Sabrina would want to know, and Elamina could deduce a lot from a simple list of ingredients, of that she was sure. What she wasn't sure about was whether she'd tell her aunt what she knew. Either way, knowledge was power. She reached for a quill and parchment. "Of course, Delia. What do you need?"

As Delia listed the ingredients, Elamina's suspicions grew. Each item was linked to the ocean, to the ebb and flow of tides and the mysteries of the deep. She scribbled down the list, her mind piecing together the puzzle.

"This potion, it's connected to the sea, isn't it?" Elamina asked nonchalantly. "It wouldn't happen to be the muirgheilt potion, would it?"

There was a brief pause on the other end. "Yes, that's the

one," Delia confirmed with a hint of surprise in her voice. "How did you know?"

Elamina leaned back in her chair, a small smile playing on her lips. "Let's just say I have my ways. It's a powerful potion, Delia. Tied to the essence of the sea itself. I'll see if I can find the ingredients and send them over, but be careful. The ocean's magic is not to be trifled with."

"Thank you, Elamina. I'll be careful, I promise," Delia replied, her tone serious.

As the communication ended, Elamina stared at the list before her. The muirgheilt potion was no small undertaking. She hoped her cousin knew what she was doing.

Curiosity piqued, Elamina wondered what Delia was up to, what need drove her to seek out such a potent and dangerous potion. She decided to keep a close eye on the situation. After all, in the world of magic and politics, knowledge was power, and Elamina intended to remain at the heart of both.

Several hours later, Elamina navigated through the grand corridors of her family's mansion, her footsteps echoing on the marble floors. The air was thick with the scent of old magic and secrets. She made her way to the ingredient storeroom, a veritable treasure trove of rare and powerful components collected over generations.

As she opened the storeroom door, her Aunt Sabrina appeared at the other end of the corridor. "What are you up to, Elamina?" she demanded, her eyes sharp and penetrating.

Elamina met her aunt's gaze with a calm she didn't entirely feel. "Building trust with our newest ally," she replied smoothly, stepping into the storeroom.

Aunt Sabrina's expression darkened. "You didn't do what I asked, and I'll seek no more favours from you, but stay away from that impostor," she hissed. "She's dangerous. And don't think I don't know about your role in rescuing her. She should be locked up back in the Clochar where she can't do any damage."

Elamina selected a vial from a shelf, her movements deliberate. "You and I have different ways of doing things, Aunt Sabrina," she said, her voice steady. "But rest assured, I have the good of the family at heart."

Sabrina scrutinised her, searching for any hint of deceit. "Your ways are reckless, Elamina. You play a dangerous game."

Elamina turned, holding the vial up to the light. "It's a game of chess, not draughts, Auntie. And sometimes, the best move is to build a bridge, not burn it."

Sabrina snorted derisively but said nothing more. She turned and stalked away.

Alone again, Elamina took a deep breath, steadying herself. Aligning with Delia was a strategic move, one that she believed would benefit the family in the long run. Her methods might differ from her aunt's, but her commitment to their legacy was unyielding.

With the necessary ingredients gathered, Elamina left the storeroom, her mind already plotting the next moves in the intricate play of politics and power. Building trust with Delia was a risk, perhaps, but Elamina was no stranger to risks. They were the currency she traded in, and she intended to emerge victorious.

43
DELIA

Delia stood with Agatha and Marjie in the cosy and spacious Thorn Manor kitchen, a sense of anticipation hanging in the air as they leaned over the table to examine the rare collection of oceanic ingredients that had just arrived in a neatly wrapped package. Elamina had come through, just like Rosemary said she would, and Delia was grateful, though a part of her wondered what kind of favour she might be expected to pay in return.

Delia had excitedly unwrapped the parcel minutes earlier and it now lay open on the kitchen table, its contents meticulously arranged inside a compartmentalised box. Delia couldn't help but marvel at the exotic array of items – the rare seaweed and salts that sparkled like tiny stars, and shells that hummed as if carrying the essence of the deep sea. The smell of brine and mystery filled the room, and Delia felt as if the ocean itself had been brought into Thorn Manor.

Delia held up a vial containing the seahorse pearls, their iridescence catching the soft kitchen light, drawing awed murmurs from her companions. "These look almost too magical to use," she commented, rolling the vial between her fingers. "I half expect them to float away before we even start."

Marjie leaned in for a closer look. "Well, what do you think, Agatha? Are these pearls filled with air like your head?" she joked, nodding towards Agatha, who was gingerly prodding a small sachet of the dark, fine powder.

By way of response, Agatha glared at Marjie. "Better to be full of air than retaining water, I'd wager." She returned her attention to the shimmering dust. "I've read about this in the many books, but seeing it in person is something else. It's said to be harvested from coral that blooms only in complete darkness, miles beneath the ocean's surface."

Ingrid began started arranging the other ingredients on the table. "Let's make sure everything is accounted for before we dive into the deep end of potion-making. We can't have your foolish banter getting in the way of a good potion."

"Here you go," Rosemary said, entering the room, carrying a large well-worn cauldron. "This was Granny's, of course. I'm sure she'd be happy to lend it to you."

Marjie smiled. "Indeed, I only wish old Galdie was here to whip us into shape. She was famous for her potions, far and wide, and this old pot has clearly seen many a brew in its time."

Delia helped Rosemary with the cauldron, placing it atop the stove, ready to be filled with the concoction they were about to create.

As they began the process, following the recipe from Marjie's grimoire, Delia found herself swept up in the rhythm of the potion-making as she measured out water and chopped the fresh seaweed they'd harvested into tiny strips.

Each ingredient was added with care, the ocean's bounty melding together in a symphony of scents and textures. The whole house seemed to come alive with the aroma of the sea, a tangible reminder of the power they were harnessing.

As Delia stirred the cauldron, a fine mist began to rise, swirling with the scent of the ocean. "Remember, it's all in the wrist," Marjie reminded her. "Don't let anything get stuck to the bottom."

"Marjie's learned that lesson the hard way," Agatha said with a chuckle.

Ingrid carefully measured out the abyssal coral dust. She dusted her hands, a cloud of coral making her sneeze. "Bless me – these must be from the sneeziest reefs in the abyss."

Agatha, leaning against the counter, watched the pearl dissolve with a faint glow. "Careful not to let any of that dust get away, Ingrid. Wouldn't want to explain to the local fish why they're feeling particularly mystical today."

"Or to the local land beings why they're feeling especially fishy!" Marjie added.

The laughter that followed was cut short as the potion began to bubble, the ingredients melding into a shimmering liquid that mirrored the colours of deep ocean waves. Delia paused her stirring and stepped back. "If I start sprouting scales, promise you'll tell Gilly and the kids that I went out in a blaze of glory – or a splash of glory, I suppose."

"In a splash, indeed," Marjie said, then she began to chant softly, weaving their laughter and camaraderie into the fabric of the spell, ensuring the potion was as potent in magic as it was rich in their shared mirth.

At one point, as Delia stirred the bubbling mixture, she closed her eyes and listened. She could have sworn she heard the gentle lapping of waves, a soothing sound that seemed to echo from the very walls of the manor. It was as if the potion was singing a song of the ocean.

As Delia continued to stir the potion, her mind drifted to Declan. She remembered their first proper meeting on the beach in Myrtlewood, the way the sea breeze had played with his hair, the mystery in his eyes. He had given her his name, but beyond that, she knew so little about him. His presence had been enigmatic, yet undeniably captivating. She'd been afraid of him then, and deeply untrusting – for good reason. She wondered now, after so much had changed, could she really trust him? She still knew so little about him, yet she felt, at some level, that they understood each other deeply – or was that just the infatuation at play?

Now, with Declan gone, a sense of longing washed over her. She wondered when, or if, he would return. Their connection had seemed almost star-crossed, a thought that made Delia smile wryly to herself. She was far too old for such fanciful notions, or so she told herself. He was a wandering rogue tracker, and she...she was a recently retired grandmother who lived in a cottage and was dipping her toes into community theatre!

What had her life become? The question lingered in her

mind as she gazed into the bubbling cauldron. Her life had taken such an unexpected turn since moving to Myrtlewood. The tranquillity of her cottage, the outrageous adventures and dangers, the deepening bonds with her fellow witches, and the unexpected stirrings of her heart – it was all so far from the life she had known just a short time before.

And yet, as she reflected on the recent weeks, Delia realised she had rarely been happier. Myrtlewood had brought her a sense of belonging, magical empowerment, and thrilling adventure.

Declan, with all his mystery and his fleeting presence, had added a layer of intrigue and emotion that she hadn't anticipated. His absence left a void.

As the potion neared completion, Delia's thoughts returned to the present, to the task at hand and the company of her friends. There were more important things to think about than mysterious men, after all.

44
AGATHA

"How do we even know this is the right ocean?" Agatha grumbled. It was a freezing cold morning and she found herself trudging towards the beach, her mood as frosty as the air around her.

"It's the sea by Myrtlewood," said Marjie. "It makes the most sense."

"That's right," said Ingrid. "And all signs in the grimoires point to here, as far as I can tell."

Agatha had never been fond of early mornings, and the biting cold did nothing to improve her disposition. The idea of venturing into the frigid ocean, armed with nothing but a potion, seemed like madness.

Marjie wrapped her arms around herself looking pale and slightly terrified. "I just hope this potion works. I'm not exactly a fan of deep water – let alone when it's freezing cold!"

Delia gave her a reassuring pat on the back. "Neither am I.

But just think of how satisfying a warm bath will be afterwards."

Ingrid was undeterred by their apprehension. "Stop dilly dallying and let's get on with it."

Agatha rolled her eyes. "Famous last words, Ingrid. Famous last words."

As they prepared to take the potion, Agatha couldn't help but grumble about the whole situation. "Next time, let's pick an adventure that requires us to stay indoors. Preferably near a fireplace with a bottle of sherry or three."

Ingrid laughed, handing Agatha a vial of the potion. "Where's your sense of excitement, Agatha? Facing the unknown with the force of our empowerment is what being a witch is all about."

Agatha took the vial reluctantly, eyeing both the potion and the ocean in the background with distrust. "Excitement is overrated. I prefer my adventures with less hypothermia risk involved."

Marjie, holding her own vial, tried to muster a smile. "Well, here's to hoping we don't turn into ice sculptures."

Delia raised her vial. "To bravery and hot baths afterwards," she declared, clearly trying to lighten the mood.

"Next time we need rare ingredients, can we make sure they're located somewhere warm? Like a desert, or a nice cosy volcano?" Agatha quipped.

Ingrid shook her head, "Oh, come on, Agatha. A little cold water is hardly a challenge when you're a powerful Crone. Think of it as a...refreshing start to the day!"

Marjie hugged herself for warmth. "If by 'refreshing' you

mean ‘turning into an ice lolly’, then yes, absolutely refreshing.”

Delia smiled. “Just imagine the stories we’ll be able to tell. ‘That time we had an underwater adventure’– it has a nice ring to it, doesn’t it?”

Agatha raised an eyebrow. “I’d prefer ‘that time we stayed in and had a nice cup of tea’. Much less risk of frostbite.”

“For once, I’m with Agatha,” Marjie said, flashing her a small smile.

“What is the world coming to!” Agatha said, throwing up her hands.

45
DELIA

Standing on the chilly beach with her potion vial in hand, Delia watched as Marjie, her face pale and hands trembling from the cold, carefully unfolded a piece of old parchment. The parchment looked fragile, its edges worn.

"What's that?" Agatha asked, her eyes narrowing.

“It's the chant that activates the potion,” Marjie said.

Marjie, her voice barely above a whisper against the sound of the waves, explained, "This fell out of the grimoire after I accidentally spilled that tea on it." She pointed to a line of tiny cursive writing along the edge of the parchment. "It says, 'Take me to the ocean and let me bathe.”

“Why didn't you show us this before?” Delia asked.

Marjie shrugged. “I suppose I was hoping for a way around all this ocean stuff at the time. I slipped it back into the book and tried to forget about it – and I was so successful I only remembered it again this morning!”

Delia laughed. “Well, thank goodness you did. It sounds important.”

Marjie sighed. “I suppose it is.”

"Well, what are you waiting for?" Ingrid asked.

Delia watched, holding her breath, as Marjie cautiously approached the water's edge. The ocean lapped gently at the shore, the frothy waves bit at her ankles. With a hesitant motion, Marjie dipped the parchment into the cold ocean water.

At first, nothing happened, and Delia felt a twinge of disappointment. But then, as the water soaked into the fibres of the parchment, something remarkable occurred. The paper, once small, plain, and unassuming, began to grow and transform. Faint blue lines and markings started to emerge, growing clearer and more defined as the parchment absorbed the sea water.

Delia gasped in surprise. “A map!”

Indeed, a map was slowly revealing itself, intricate and detailed. There were markings that looked like landmarks, twisting paths that resembled routes, and symbols that were undoubtedly magical in nature. The lines were delicate yet deliberate, drawn with an expertise that spoke of skilled hands.

Agatha sighed. “If you’d remembered this before, Marjie, perhaps we could have found another way to get there rather than taking a potion and diving into the sea – hoping for the best!”

Ingrid shook her head. “No. Everything happens in its right time, unless obstructed, and this is clearly the right time for this adventure. Can’t you feel it?”

A subtle shiver ran up Delia's arms at those words. *Yes, I can feel it.*

The map pulsed with energy, as if the ocean water had awakened a dormant magic within it. Delia, Marjie, Agatha, and Ingrid leaned in.

Delia felt a thrill run through her.

"Amazing!" Delia said, then her eyes flicked to the vast horizon and she caught a glimmer of light. "Look over there!"

Something was approaching; the glimmer of light on the horizon grew closer, taking form amidst the crashing waves.

Marjie's first genuine smile of the day was a beacon of reassurance. "That'll be him!"

Delia's gaze fixed on the emerging figure, a sense of awe washing over her. Through the misty sea spray, a striking figure moved gracefully through the water. He was a beautiful, broad-chested man with long, flowing hair that seemed to dance with the rhythm of the ocean. A radiant smile lit up his face with a warmth that reached far and wide.

"Hello, Mervyn!" Marjie called out with a jolly wave.

But it was the lower half of his body that left Delia speechless. From the waist down, he was unmistakably fish-like, his powerful tail gliding through the water with an effortless elegance. His scales shimmered in the morning light, reflecting a kaleidoscope of silvery blues and greens.

"A merman!" Delia blurted out, her voice betraying her shock and fascination.

Agatha cackled. "Who did you think we were meeting, Peter Pan?"

"I had an inkling," Delia mumbled, still captivated by the

merman's approach. "And you've all mentioned merfolk...but the reality is far more impressive!"

As Mervyn neared the shore, his tail propelling him through the surf with graceful strokes, the world around Delia seemed to fade. The ocean, the beach, the cold air – all of it paled in comparison to the magic unfolding before her eyes.

Agatha leaned in closer to Delia. "Quite a looker, isn't he?"

Delia elbowed her playfully as the merman reached the shallows and, with a smooth motion, lifted himself onto a rock, his tail glistening in the sun. Delia couldn't help but stare, enchanted by this mythical creature who seemed to embody the essence of the sea.

Marjie, breaking the spell, stepped forward with a warm smile. "Thank you so much for coming, Mervyn. I know you usually stay at sea until the weather warms up, but I can't tell you how much I appreciate your help. We're honoured by your presence."

Mervyn bowed his head slightly. "The honour is mine, Marjie. The Crones' power is legendary. The ocean has whispered of your quest and I am pleased to play a part, no matter how small."

"Everyone, this is Mervyn," Marjie said. "He's agreed to help us with our quest."

Marjie introduced him to Ingrid and Delia, who'd never had the pleasure. "And I suppose you've met Agatha before?" she added. "Given that you've both spent a substantial time in Myrtlewood village."

Agatha shrugged. "I've never been much for ice cream, but

I've seen you around. Though...never in such an impressive form."

Mervyn smiled sheepishly. "I prefer to blend in when I'm working during the summers, otherwise people get excited about more than just the ice cream parlour and it gets... complicated."

Delia noticed a blush creeping over his cheeks. "Well, thank you so much for helping us," she added, bringing the conversation back on track.

Mervyn nodded graciously, his eyes sparkling like the ocean. "It's rare to aid in such a venture. I'm intrigued by your courage."

Agatha quipped, "Well, courage or madness, the jury's still out on that one."

Delia chuckled along with the others.

"What do we do now?" Marjie asked.

"I see you have the potion," Mervyn said. "So, now...well, I suppose you need to get into the sea."

They then began removing their shoes and stockings; the cold sand beneath Delia's feet was a sharp reminder of the task ahead.

As they tentatively waded into the freezing water, Delia shivered, the chill biting at her toes and creeping up her legs. When they were knee deep. Mervyn announced that it was time to take the potion.

"Cheers," Delia muttered as she held the potion vial up.

They each took a deep breath before downing the contents. Delia braced herself, expecting an immediate transformation, but instead, there was a moment of stillness, as if the sea itself was holding its breath.

Then, it began. Instead of the icy chill of the ocean, a warmth spread through Delia's body, countering the cold water. It started at her feet and slowly spiralled upwards, along with a tingling sensation, exhilarating and disconcerting.

She sighed as a delightfully pleasant feeling like the gentle lapping of cool waves on a hot summer's day spread through her body.

She watched in awe her legs began to shimmer, the transformation subtle at first but growing more pronounced by the second.

Her clothing faded and then vanished to be replaced by something far more strange. The skin of her legs took on a pearly-red sheen, fusing and reshaping, until a magnificent tail took form, red scales glinting in the morning light, forming into intricate jewelled shell-like patterns that covered her chest. The colours were mesmerising – a rich, vibrant crimson with amber and vermillion tones, each scale edged with darker hues, giving the appearance of a fiery flow, deep and intense, like the heart of a flame.

"Is everyone else seeing this?" Delia asked, half in wonder, half in disbelief.

Agatha, now sporting a tail of her own, a rich yellow and silver, laughed. "If we're hallucinating, then it's a collective one!"

The sensation of having a tail was alien yet strangely natural. Delia moved deeper into the water as she experimented with a few swishes, marvelling at the powerful movements that sent ripples through the water.

The transformation was complete.

“We’re mermaids!” Marjie crowed, her previous fear replaced by astonished glee as she examined at her own tail. The scales transitioned from a pale sky blue at the top to a rich, dark navy at the fin. It looked as if it was carved from the ocean itself, a harmonious blend of various shades of blue that rippled with the water's ebb and flow. It was as if Marjie had become one with the sea, her tail a part of the vast, endless blue. "This is incredible. We're really doing this."

Ingrid laughed and dove into the water, her tail splashing playfully. "Come on, our ocean adventure awaits!"

Ingrid's tail was a vibrant emerald green, each scale shimmering like a jewel under the sun. The scales overlapped gracefully, catching the light with every movement, reminiscent of the lush, deep forests of the sea. Her tail moved effortlessly through the water, leaving a trail of green hues that danced in the morning light.

Delia took a deep breath, feeling a connection to the sea she had never known before. With a final glance at the shore, she dove in, the water embracing her in a way it never had. They were no longer just witches; for now, at least, they were creatures of the ocean, embarking on a journey into the unknown.

46
MARJIE

Bobbing in the water, Marjie felt a knot of trepidation in her stomach. Her transformation into a mermaid had been magnificent, but as the thrill wore off she realised that though her new temporary form made the cold water much more bearable, it did little to ease her long-standing fear of the ocean depths. She watched the waves lap gently at the shore, longing for the safe stability of dry land.

"I wonder how long this will last," Delia said, flicking her fiery-toned tail. "It's brilliant, but I suppose we don't want to permanently be half-fish."

Agatha cackled with her arms behind her head, resting casually on a small cresting wave. "Speak for yourself. I could live like this."

"It's supposed to be for half a day," Marjie said nervously. "But as soon as we get back to the shore it will wear off. It only works in the ocean."

As she gazed at her new blue tail, shimmering and elegant, Marjie couldn't deny the marvel of their transformation. The scales caught the light, creating patterns that reminded her of the sky on a clear summer's day. Yet, the beauty of it couldn't quite shake the anxiety that gripped her.

"Come on, Marjie, the water's calling!" Ingrid called out, as she dived back into the sea, her emerald green tail flicking water playfully.

Marjie swam forward slowly. "It's not the water I'm worried about," she muttered under her breath. "It's the terrifying mystery of what's in it."

Agatha laughed. "What, afraid of a few fish, Marjie?"

"It's not the fish, Agatha," Marjie replied, her voice tinged with nervousness. "It's the enormous vastness. It's...overwhelming."

Delia offered a comforting smile. "We're all in this together, Marjie. Besides, we've faced scarier things than a bit of water."

Marjie nodded, drawing strength from Delia's words. She took a deep breath and swam deeper, so that her tail could no longer flick against the soft sand below. The sensation of floating without touching the bottom was disorienting at first, but slowly, a sense of wonder began to replace her fear.

As the four Crones ventured further into the ocean, the water embracing their new forms, Marjie's trepidation gave way to a cautious curiosity. The sea around them was alive with colour and movement, a world so different from the one she knew on land.

Agatha sent a small wave towards Marjie and she splashed back with her tail.

"Look at you, Marjie, a natural mermaid!" Ingrid chuckled.

"I wouldn't go that far," Marjie replied, a hint of a smile on her lips. "But I suppose it's not too bad."

As they swam deeper into the vast expanse of the ocean, Marjie felt a cocktail of emotions churning within her. The element of water was both her close ally and her great fear. As she swam with her fellow Crones, her new mermaid form gliding gracefully through the water, she tried to focus her mind, and quickly found herself seeking solace in thoughts of Papa Jack. His soothing voice, a steadfast presence in her life, echoed in her mind, calming her racing heart.

"Remember, it's just another adventure," she imagined him saying, his words a balm to her anxious soul.

"Marjie," Delia said. "You still haven't put your head under. Come on..."

Marjie took a deep breath and, despite her fears, dove deep into the sea. Of course, she was expecting it, but it still surprised her to find she could breathe underwater. The sensation was both bizarre and exhilarating. Each breath was a marvel, the water filling her lungs not with dread, but with life. The fear of deep water still lingered, but the magic of their transformation lent her a courage she hadn't known she possessed.

Around her, Agatha, Delia, and Ingrid revelled in their newfound forms. Their voices, when they spoke, came out in melodic tones, like songs of the sea, but somehow comprehensible. The music of their voices was enchanting as they swam further towards the light that beckoned them.

It was Mervyn. He'd disappeared below the surface shortly

after they'd taken the potion, satisfied that it worked. Now he was guiding them, just as he'd promised.

Delia called out in a sing-song voice, "Look at us, the sirens of Myrtlewood! Who would have thought?"

"No, no," Agatha grumbled, melodically. "Sirens are nasty business. Totally different. We don't want to mess with them."

As they swam, Marjie allowed herself to enjoy the sensations because doing so eased her fear. The sway of her gorgeous blue tail felt natural, the cool water caressing her skin. Schools of fish darted around them, curious yet unafraid, their scales glinting like tiny jewels. The ocean's colours were more vivid than she had ever imagined, the marine life offering a plethora of shapes and hues.

Marjie felt a sense of wonder overtaking her. The ocean was a world of its own, vast and mysterious, yet here she was, a part of it. Her friends' laughter and song-like voices filled the water in melodic harmony.

47
INGRID

As Ingrid propelled herself through the water, the thrill of being a mermaid filled her with an exuberant joy, so unlike her ordinary emotional state that the difference alone was thrilling. Her emerald green tail, fluid and powerful, cut through the ocean with graceful ease. The water around her was a world alive with wonders, the sunlight filtering through the waves, casting dancing patterns on the sea floor below.

The ocean's vastness, which had initially seemed daunting even if Ingrid wouldn't have admitted it, now felt like a playground of endless possibilities. Schools of fish swam past, seemingly curious about these new visitors. Ingrid laughed, a sound that bubbled melodically through the water, as a particularly bold fish darted close, as if to inspect her shimmering scales.

"Here come the unlikely mermaids of Myrtlewood," Ingrid called out to her companions, her voice a harmonious echo in the deep. "Who would've thought we'd be swimming with the fishes, quite literally!"

Agatha, her bright yellow tail shining bright against the deep blue, responded with a wry grin. "I always fancied myself more of a bird than a fish. But I must admit, this isn't half bad."

Marjie, her blue tail flicking nervously yet beautifully in the water, added, "As long as we don't run into any sharks, I suppose I'll manage."

Delia, elegant with her red tail, chimed in, "Well, if we do, we'll just have to charm them with our newfound mermaid grace. Or send Agatha to negotiate."

As they followed Mervyn's glowing light, the sea around them deepened in colour, the blues growing richer, the world beneath the waves unveiling its secrets.

Ingrid felt a sense of liberation, her worries and doubts dissolving in the saline waters. Here, in the embrace of the ocean, she was not just a witch or a Crone; she was a temporary creature of the sea. The sensation of freedom was exhilarating along with the movements that felt both alien and surprisingly natural.

The oceanic wonderland around her was clearly a magical place, perhaps hidden by enchantment from mundane eyes. The pinks, purples, and bluey-green colours of the coral and stone had an otherworldly glow to them.

As they ventured deeper, Ingrid caught her first glimpse of the underwater society. It was a city unlike any she had seen. From a distance, it was reminiscent of the Clochar in which she'd grown up, but submerged and thriving beneath the waves. The architecture was both majestic and organic, buildings that seemed to be carved from coral and stone, adorned with sea plants that swayed gently in the current.

"Why are you taking us here?" Ingrid asked, her voice a melodic ripple in the water.

Mervyn turned, his eyes serious yet filled with a sense of purpose. "You journey here only at the pleasure of the King of the Sea, King Lir. He awaits your audience."

Ingrid exchanged nervous glances with Marjie, Delia, and Agatha. The idea of meeting an underwater king was daunting, but it seemed they had no choice but to follow the protocol.

Mervyn led them through magnificent underwater archways, each one more elaborate than the last. The sea plants that decorated them glowed softly, illuminating their path with an ethereal light. The path they followed was long and glowing, snaking its way towards the heart of the underwater city.

Ingrid's excitement mingled with a growing sense of nervousness. The grandeur of their surroundings was now overwhelming, the realisation of where they were, and whom they were about to meet, suddenly very real.

Agatha, swimming alongside Ingrid, whispered jokingly, "If I'd known we were meeting royalty, I would have worn my best pearls."

Delia chuckled. "I'm not sure anything we own would pass for court fashion here."

Marjie glanced around nervously. "As long as we don't have to curtsy...I wouldn't know how to with a tail!"

As they swam closer, Ingrid's heart raced faster. What would King Lir be like? What did he know about their quest?

And what role did they have to play in the grand scheme of the sea?

The royal palace drew nearer, a sprawling structure that seemed to be carved from the ocean floor, and Mervyn halted, turning to them with a solemn expression. "Prepare yourselves," he said. "The King of the Sea awaits."

As they paused at the threshold of the palace, the enormity of the moment settled upon Ingrid. This was it – the point of no return. What lay beyond those grand doors was unknown, and Ingrid couldn't help but wonder if they were ready to face whatever was to come.

48
AGATHA

Agatha flipped gleefully through the ocean. The initial unease surrounding this whole under-sea venture had transformed with the first flick of her yellow tail through the water. The sensation undeniably strange but also thrilling. Each flick and swirl of her new appendage propelled her forward with surprising speed, which both delighted and unnerved her.

Agatha couldn't help but marvel at the underwater world unfurling before her eyes as they swam deeper. The ocean was a veritable cauldron of life and colour, a realm so different from the land she knew. The sea floor was a mosaic of corals and sea plants, swaying gently with the current.

As they neared the underwater palace, Agatha's awe grew. She wished she had some way to document everything. Books and writings on this realm were rare and not believed to be entirely accurate, and her inner-scholar itched to make a few corrections to the record, but that would have to wait. There were more urgent things to accomplish.

The structure rose from the ocean floor, its architecture a harmonious blend of natural formations and deliberate artistry. Towers of coral, windows framed with intricately woven kelp, and archways adorned with shells and pearls made it seem as if the palace had grown organically from the seabed itself, a sight that rendered Agatha momentarily speechless.

“You’re oddly quiet,” Marjie said, nudging Agatha with her tail. “It’s making me more nervous.”

"Well, I must say, this is remarkable," Agatha said, her voice carrying a note of wonder.

Ingrid laughed. "If that’s the only remark Agatha can make, it’s really something special."

Delia sighed in awe, her red tail a vivid streak against the ocean's palette. “It’s just like something I would have dreamed of as a young girl.”

Agatha felt a deeper throb of excitement and nervousness, as they drew nearer. It was the stuff of childhood imaginings indeed, except in this case, it was far more real and dangerous. The underwater palace was like something out of a storybook. She wondered what the King of the Sea would be like, and what awaited them within those coral walls. Rumours suggested he was a fair ruler, but also formidable.

Agatha found herself embracing the experience. The ocean, with all its mysteries and wonders, had a way of putting things into perspective, reminding her that magic was not just spell books and potions, but the extraordinary moments shared with friends in the heart of the unknown.

As they followed Mervyn along the glowing path towards the grand entrance of the underwater palace, she couldn't help but marvel at the sights around them. "Well, if I had known in advance we'd be attending a royal audience, I might have brushed my hair. Or at least found a seaweed wreath to wear."

Delia giggled. "Agatha, I don't think the fish mind your hairstyle. Though I hear sea urchin accessories are all the rage this season down here."

Marjie joined in the laughter, though nervously. "I just hope there's no dress code. I'd hate to be turned away for inappropriate tail attire."

Ingrid nudged Agatha gently. "I think our mermaid forms are quite the fashion statement already. Besides, I doubt King Lir gets many land-walkers turned merfolk visiting. We'll be the talk of the ocean."

The merfolk they passed seemed to pay them no mind, going about their business with an elegance that only deepened the surreal nature of their adventure.

"Look at that," Delia pointed out, as a particularly colourful merman swam by, his scales shimmering with a thousand different hues. "I wonder if he offers fashion tips."

Agatha snorted, amused despite herself. "I'm more curious about Marjie's question from earlier. Will we need to curtsy? How does one even curtsy with a mermaid tail?"

"Like this, obviously. Graceful as always." Ingrid, attempting a mock curtsy in the water, nearly lost her balance, causing a ripple of laughter to spread through the group.

Joking aside, Agatha did wonder whether they should have devised more of a strategy. Mervyn was a wealth of information, yet he'd told them very little.

As they made their way through the grand entrance of the underwater palace, the scale and beauty of their surroundings deepened their sense of awe.

The water around them was clearer here, imbued with an ethereal light that seemed to emanate from the sea bed itself. The path led to an enormous archway adorned with intricate carvings of sea life, pearls and precious stones embedded into the walls casting shimmering reflections that danced across their path.

As they entered an enormous and grand throne room, Agatha took a deep breath. The splendour of the underwater palace truly revealed itself. The ceiling soared overhead, supported by pillars that spiralled like giant shells. The floor was a mosaic of coloured stones, depicting scenes of the ocean's majesty. Schools of elegant fish swam in patterns above them, their movements synchronised in a mesmerising display.

At the far end of the room with a commanding presence, sat an enormous merman, obviously King Lir.

Seated on a throne of pearl and coral, and flanked by strong merfolk on each side, the King was clearly powerful, his gaze piercing through the water with an intensity that was grand and terrifying.

Mervyn bowed deeply. "My King, I present to you, my friends, the powerful Crones of Myrtlewood. They have an important mission to attend to in your realm."

King Lir regarded them for a moment before speaking, his voice deep and resonant, echoing through the chamber. "Visitors of the land above, to seek my audience, you must prove your worth. Answer me this riddle: I am not alive, but I grow; I don't have lungs, but I need air; I don't have a mouth, but water kills me. What am I?"

The Crones huddled together, whispering among themselves.

Ingrid's brow furrowed in concentration, "Not alive, but grows? Needs air? This sounds like something from a gardener's nightmare."

Marjie added, "Well, it's certainly not a fish. Or any of us, now that we're in mer-state."

Delia made a poor attempt to lighten the mood. "Perhaps it's a trick question. Maybe he's talking about a mermaid's hairdo."

Agatha had been quietly mulling over the riddle, then suddenly snapped her fingers, a spark of realisation in her eyes. "It's fire! Fire grows, needs air, but water extinguishes it."

The group turned back to King Lir, and Agatha stepped forward. "Your Majesty, the answer to your riddle is fire."

King Lir's stern expression softened into a smile, the tension in the room dissipating like mist. "Well answered," he declared, his deep voice now carrying a note of approval. "You have proven your worth. What is it that you seek in my realm?"

Relief washed over Agatha, along with a little thrill of accomplishment. They had passed the King's test, but their journey was far from over. The mysteries of the deep awaited them, and their adventure in the underwater realm was only just beginning.

49
MARJIE

Trembling before King Lir in the grandeur of his underwater palace, Marjie felt the weight of her mission pressing down on her. They'd passed the first test – with Agatha's brilliant mind, they'd solved the King's riddle, but now came the hard part.

Marjie gathered her courage and addressed the king with a sincerity that came from the depth of her soul.

"Your Majesty, we come before you to ask for your permission to venture into your kingdom for a particular quest. Our mission is of the utmost importance, not just to us, personally, but for our village, and far further afield. Indeed, dark powers are awakening that could threaten the entire world..." Marjie implored, her voice steady despite the tremor of fear in her heart.

King Lir regarded her with a gaze as deep and unfathomable as the ocean itself. "What care I for the world above ground?" he scoffed, his voice echoing through the throne room. "The affairs of the land dwellers are of no concern to me."

Marjie's heart sank, but she pressed on, desperation lending her voice strength. "But, Your Majesty, it's not just the land that's at risk. Even your vast ocean could be in danger. We must act to protect it all."

The king's expression was unreadable, his eyes reflecting the distant light of his realm. For a moment, silence filled the room. “Are you implying that I cannot protect my own realm?”

“Not at all,” Marjie said. “But please—”

The King cut her off with a wave of his hand. "Leave my sight. Your concerns are not mine to share."

Disheartened, Marjie turned to leave, her hopes dashed.

But Delia and Ingrid were by her side in an instant, their determination unshaken. "Try again, Marjie. He needs to understand how crucial this is," Delia whispered.

Ingrid nodded. "We can't give up now. Not when we've come so far."

Agatha gripped her arm. “Marjie, you’re a powerful Crone – you’re the most empathic person I’ve ever known. Speak from the heart. Let your blasted intuition guide you the way you always insist I do the same.”

Marjie suppressed a small smile at Agatha’s words. It was true, she always gave such sage advice because it tended to help. Perhaps now it was time to take some of her own medicine.

Taking a deep breath, Marjie faced King Lir once more, her companions' encouragement fuelling her resolve. The king's stern gaze met hers as she pleaded their case again, her heart laid bare before him. She told him her story – using the words that emerged from deep within.

After what felt like an eternity, King Lir finally spoke. "Very well. You have shown much courage, witch. Speaking from the heart is brave indeed. I do not share your concerns of these threats, however, I grant you permission to proceed with your mission," he declared, his voice resonating through the water. "But on one condition – you may take only memories with you from my domain. Do not remove anything belonging to the ocean. Not a single stone or shell."

Relief washed over Marjie, mingled with a new sense of foreboding.

Permission to continue was welcome news indeed, yet the condition imposed by the king was a lead weight in her gut. Their mission required them to retrieve the water dragon, in whatever form she might take, a task that now seemed even more daunting with the King's heavy decree.

She glanced anxiously towards Mervyn, wondering whether she ought to voice her doubts – to mention that they must retrieve something precious indeed – but the friendly merman shook his head, his posture rigid.

Marjie exhaled, then bowed deeply and thanked King Lir, understanding that to complicate matters now would put them all at great risk – so too would their betrayal, but they could worry about that later.

As they swam away, Marjie reassured herself. The water dragon, a creature of myth and legend, surely didn't belong to any one domain. Dragons were beings of their own, free and boundless.

"Dragons belong to themselves," she whispered, trying to quell the rising doubt within her.

Moments later, guided by the ancient map that had fallen from her grimoire, Marjie and Mervyn led the way through the vast underwater world, with the other Crones close behind. The map's intricate lines and symbols wove a path through the ocean's depths.

Towering underwater mountains rose from the sea floor, their peaks shrouded in seaweed and shy schools of fish. Deep valleys teemed with vibrant coral forests. The light from above filtered down in ghostly beams, illuminating their way.

"Think of all the boring meetings we could avoid if we stayed down here." Agatha chuckled, her voice bubbling through the water.

Delia laughed. "And imagine the parties, Agatha! An underwater ballroom, with coral chandeliers and fish flitting through. We could serve plankton pâté!"

"And seaweed wraps on the side," Ingrid added with a smirk, floating effortlessly beside them, her arms crossed as if she were lounging rather than swimming.

Agatha, who had been scouting a particularly lush coral outcrop, called back to them, her voice clear and excited. "And don't forget the treasure! Who knows what secrets these waters hide? Ancient shipwrecks, forgotten realms..."

Mervyn eyed them warily. "I know you're joking, but please do remember what the King said. Take only memories."

Marjie's heart was heavy with dread. Each flick of her tail

brought her closer to her greatest fear – the deep, darkness that awaited them which gnawed at her soul. Being on the ocean floor was terrifying enough but going even deeper?

The map was clear; the water dragon was hidden in the heart of the ocean, beyond a chasm that plunged into the abyss. The thought of venturing into those unfathomable depths, into the darkness where the pressure of the water threatened to crush her very soul, filled her with a terror she could hardly bear.

Her fears came to a head as they arrived at the edge of the chasm. The abyss yawned before them, a gaping maw that seemed to swallow the light, an entrance to a world untouched by the sun.

The company of the Crones had kept her from completely being overtaken by her icy terror, but now, new text appeared, scrawling itself in silver lettering across the map.

Only one may enter her lair.

Only the true Crone of water may draw near.

Mervyn gave Marjie a solemn look as he eyed the writing. She knew in her heart that it was true. She must go down alone.

The realisation struck her with the force of a tsunami.

"I...I have to go down there?" Marjie's voice was barely a whisper, her gaze fixed on the darkness below.

"Yes," Mervyn replied, his voice gentle but firm. "The water dragon awaits. Only you can enter."

The crones gathered around Marjie, offering words of encouragement.

Delia patted her on the shoulder. "You're braver than you know. You've got this, Marjie. We believe in you."

“Just think of it as a mud puddle – like on winter solstice night,” Ingrid added. “It might feel odd at first, but it’s not all that unpleasant once you’re in it.”

"Just think of it as diving into a really deep bathtub. You'll be fine," Agatha quipped.

Marjie turned back towards the abyss and then hesitated.

"If you find any lost treasures down there, Marjie, remember who your favourite crone is," Agatha said, winking. The lightness in her tone, buoyant, against the serious weight of the situation.

Marjie took a deep breath and felt the words of her good friends wrapping around her like a warm embrace, fortifying her resolve.

With a deep breath, Marjie summoned every ounce of courage she possessed. She nodded to her friends, a silent goodbye, before turning to face the chasm.

As she began her descent, the ocean revealed its secrets in layers. The light from above faded, giving way to the deep blue of the midwater, where jellyfish danced like ethereal ballerinas.

As she descended further into the abyss, the darkness enveloped her, the cold seeping into her bones. Her heart raced, her fears magnified by the silence and the isolation.

The deeper Marjie went, the more the pressure of the ocean weighed upon her, a physical reminder of the burden she carried. Yet, with each stroke of her tail, she felt the strength of her convictions pushing her onward, a counterbalance to the weight of the sea.

As she surrendered to her journey, the abyss became not just a place of fear, but also of wonder. The darkness enveloped her more and more, and Marjie realised that the ocean's depths were much like the unknown paths of life – terrifying to behold, but filled with potential for beauty and discovery. It was a lesson she would carry with her, a reminder that courage was not the absence of fear, but the choice to face it.

Guided by her intuition, and the map's magic, Marjie felt a change within her. The terror that had threatened to overwhelm her transformed into a fierce determination.

She was a descendant of a long line of powerful witches, and she would not be defeated by fear.

Finally, as she reached the bottom of the chasm, Marjie found herself in a cavern of unimaginable beauty. Bioluminescent plants cast a soft glow, revealing patterns...a face...

The water dragon was right there – before her.

Marjie gasped as she took in the truly majestic sight of the dragon, her scales shimmering with all the colours of the ocean.

In that moment of awe, Marjie knew exactly what to do.

She'd already faced her fears in coming this far; now, all she had to do was let go her defences and open her heart. She let the tension leave her body and allowed her eyes to take in the full glory of the water dragon.

Facing her deepest fears had led her to this wondrous creature and she had no way of protecting herself now, other than surrendering to the deep ancient being before her.

Marjie bowed her head, slowly, then rolled back her shoulders, and a beautiful sound sprang from her lips, as if echoing the music of her heart.

The water dragon regarded her with ancient, wise eyes, and a connection formed between them, a bond as deep and enduring as the ocean itself, and in that moment, the dragon vanished, to be replaced by a brilliant blue gem.

50
PAPA JACK

Papa Jack stood behind the counter, stirring slowly. The air was filled with the scent of mint and bittersweet chocolate while Rosemary planned out the next window display. They were experimenting with their refreshing peppermint truffles. The original recipe had either too much peppermint or too much magic, perhaps both, inducing a blizzard-like experience. This was an attempt at a subtler effect. As he mixed the chocolate ganache, folding in the peppermint extract according to Rosemary's instructions, Papa Jack couldn't help but feel a surge of contentment. This shop was more than just a business; it was a place where magic happened, one bite of chocolate at a time, and he was proud to be a part of it.

"Call me when you're ready for the refreshing charm," Rosemary said. "Oh...what do you think about making tiny blossoms out of white chocolate - with dark stems, of course.

Would that be too fiddly for our next display? It's getting closer to Imbolc, after all—"

"Ugh." Papa Jack bent over.

"What?" Rosemary narrowed her eyes and got up from the table. "I take it this isn't a reaction to spring blossoms?"

Papa Jack shook his head, struggling to find the right words. Amidst the rhythmic stirring and the gentle clinking of the spoon against the bowl, Papa Jack had felt a sudden, inexplicable pang of panic that knotted his stomach.

Rosemary approached and put her hand on his shoulder. "Papa Jack, what is it?"

"It's Marjie," he said, setting the spoon down with a clatter. "I can't explain it, but I feel like she's in trouble, or about to be. It's like a...a tug in my soul."

Rosemary's eyes widened. "Then we must go to her," she said decisively. "Wherever she is, whatever it is that's happening to her, she needs us."

Papa Jack hesitated, glancing around the chocolate shop, his sanctuary. "But the shop?"

"The shop can wait," Rosemary replied firmly. She walked over to the door, flipping the sign to 'Closed' with a flick of her wrist. "Family comes first. You know that better than anyone. And Marjie is family to me."

As they prepared to leave, Papa Jack glanced around to make sure everything was in order. The rows of chocolates seemed to stand in silent support. This place was a part of his home, but Marjie...Marjie was his heart.

"Let's go," he said. "And err... the situation might be more complicated than you realise."

Rosemary laughed. “It always is – Marjie should be deep in the ocean by now.”

Papa Jack smiled nervously. “I’m glad she told you about that so I didn’t have to be the one to break the news. Any idea how we’re going to get to her?”

“I suppose going to the beach is a start,” Rosemary suggested. “We can figure something out once we get there, or at least we can try. I can’t very well sit here while one of my dearest friends is in danger.”

Together, Papa Jack and Rosemary left the shop, the door closing behind them with a soft click. As they hurried through the streets of Myrtlewood, Papa Jack's thoughts were consumed by Marjie.

Racing towards the beach, Papa Jack and Rosemary found a weathered-looking man there wearing a leather hat. Rosemary introduced him as Declan, a friend of Delia’s. Marjie had mentioned this man before as somewhat of a rogue, but Papa Jack could see in his eyes that he was honourable, if troubled, standing there, solitary against the backdrop of the churning sea.

Declan's expression was grave. "Something’s wrong.”

Papa Jack. "What's happened?"

Declan shook his head. “I don’t know exactly, but I could sense it.”

“As could I,” Papa Jack said.

Rosemary nodded. “That’s why we came here. Where are they? What can we—"

Declan raised a hand. "They’re still in the ocean, but that's not the only problem. The Order of Crimson...they're on their way here."

Papa Jack gulped. Marjie had told him all about the Order and their horrendous crusade against the Crones.

"They know where the Crones are," Declan continued. "And the worst part is, everything from the shore here, out to the ocean, is out of the zone of the magical protection they set up over Myrtlewood."

The words struck Papa Jack with a force that seemed to drain the colour from the world around him.

Rosemary took a deep breath. "We need to do something. Marjie's already in danger and this is even worse. We can't let the Order capture her and the others."

Papa Jack nodded, his mind racing through the possibilities. "But we can't go into the ocean, not like this. We're not equipped to face what's down there and we have no idea what the danger is that they're facing. Nor to fight the Order up here on land."

Declan looked between them. "I'm going to do my best to help, though I don't know if my magic can reach them underwater. But either way, at least we can face the Order here, strategically. Let's prepare a welcome they weren't expecting."

The determination in Declan's voice ignited a spark of hope within Papa Jack. It was time to rally that power in defence of those they held dear.

As they began to strategize, Papa Jack couldn't help but worry for Marjie. She was out there, in the vastness of the ocean, facing dangers they could scarcely imagine. He quickly brought his attention back to the present. He had to focus and play his part, no matter how small, for Marjie's sake.

51
DELIA

Delia's heart soared as she watched Marjie emerge from the chasm, her hand tightly clutching a sapphire gem that gleamed with an inner light.

"Is that..." Agatha began.

"The water dragon's amulet," Marjie said, holding up the stone which sparkled in Marjie's grasp, its deep blue hues reflecting the ocean's depths.

A sense of triumph and relief washed over Delia.

But their moment of victory was short-lived. A disturbance rippled through the water, the calm of the ocean shattered by an urgent warning. Mervyn's voice, usually so calm and composed, was laced with panic. "Move fast! You must leave now!" he yelled, his eyes wide with alarm. "The King is coming."

Delia's heart skipped a beat as she glimpsed, in the distance, the king's guard approaching, a formidable school of mer-warriors, their tails propelling them through the water with incredible speed, armed with tridents and other sharp pointy weapons.

“Let’s go!” Delia cried.

They wasted no time, swimming away, and upward with all the powerful strength their mermaid forms could muster. The once tranquil waters had become a chaotic mess.

"Of all the underwater excursions we could have had, we get the chase scene!" Delia shouted over her shoulder.

Agatha gurgled out a laugh. "Next time, let's stick to treasure hunts on land!"

Marjie cackled, clearly high on adrenaline. "Think of the story we'll tell! 'The Great Oceanic Escape' sounds like a best-seller to me!"

Delia shook her head. "Just as long as it has a happy ending!"

“Stop bantering and get those tails moving quick spot!” Ingrid called out.

They swam as if in formation, like a pod of whales, weaving through the ocean, the beauty of their surroundings lost to the urgency of their flight. Pillars of coral and archways adorned with bioluminescent algae flashed by, their ethereal glow a beacon in the chaos.

Behind them, the king’s guard gained ground, their determination clear in the steady beat of their tails. Delia could feel the pressure of their pursuit, a constant reminder that the ocean's wonders were matched by its dangers.

Take only memories... King Lir had said, with a warning tone.

But now Marjie has the stone. He must know, somehow...He must think we're stealing from him.

Mervyn led them through a series of tight turns and narrow passages, his knowledge of the ocean's secrets their only advantage.

As the water opened up before them, Delia dared to hope they might escape, but there was still far to swim to reach dry land, and out here, they were even more vulnerable with no cover.

"There's nothing for it," said Ingrid. "We're going to have to use our magic, even if we don't know how it will work under water..."

"We really should have practiced earlier," Marjie lamented.

"No time like the present." Agatha summoned currents of swirling water, creating vortexes to momentarily disorient their pursuers.

Ingrid, with a flick of her emerald tail, caused the ocean floor to rise up and ensnare several of the guard who were still far below them.

Marjie, her focus sharp despite the chaos, sent wave after wave of strong ocean currents towards the King. He roared in protest, but struggled on towards them.

Delia tried to summon her own magic, but felt it smoulder and then extinguish – doused by the water element which was often considered its opposite.

She sighed, feeling somewhat useless.

Under the weight of their situation, she allowed panic to creep into her heart. The thought of losing everything – her family, her life, and the secret they had uncovered – was unbearable. *We can't let them catch us. Not now,* she thought frantically, the fear of their mission dying in the depths almost paralysing her. She wasn't sure why, but in that moment, she reached out to Declan in her mind. Perhaps he could hear her, or perhaps not. She had no idea if his magic would even work down here, but in her desperation, any avenue was worth pursuing.

They continued to swim away, the other Crones blasting their magic back towards the King's guard who were swiftly gaining on them. They only had moments until they were caught, but a shimmering up ahead drew Delia's attention. The water glowed with a familiar magic.

"Look!" Delia exclaimed, pointing at the swirling vortex of light and shadow.

"A portal? Now?" Agatha huffed, her voice tinged with incredulity. "Who's to say that isn't a trap?"

Ingrid, peering at the portal with scepticism, couldn't help but quip, "Well, it's not like we have a better escape plan. Unless you've got a submarine hidden somewhere, Agatha."

Marjie sighed. "Anything's better than being captured."

Delia, recognising the resonance of the portal's magic, felt a surge of hope. "It's Declan," she said, a conviction in her voice that brooked no argument. "It's his magic. Let's go."

With no time to waste Delia led the charge towards the portal, pulling the other crones with her.

"Wait," Marjie cried out. "I need a minute."

"We don't have a minute!" Delia cried.

"Give me thirty seconds, then," Marjie insisted. "We can't leave Mervyn like this – we have to make things right."

"Twenty!" said Agatha.

Marjie turned towards the king and, just as she'd known what to do when facing the water dragon, she trusted her intuition and opened up energetically to her own empathy.

A powerful wave of magic flowed out from her heart, an entirely different kind from her previous attacks.

Waves of harmonic sound echoed through the ocean, calming, empathising, beautiful and sorrowful.

Delia felt tears well up in her eyes.

King Lir stopped in his watery tracks, staring at Marjie, his eyes wide with wonder and sadness.

He held his hand to his heart and bowed his head.

Marjie turned to Mervyn. "Will you come with us?"

He bowed his head. "No, my friend. I will humble myself before my king. But thank you, your heartsong has shown him the true calling of your soul and now he understands the gravity of your mission. Go well, and I hope to see you again this summer."

"Save me some of your strawberry ripple." Marjie grinned at him then turned back to Delia. "We can go now."

Delia stared at her a moment longer, still in awe of her friend and the profound magic she'd unleashed.

Then, she grabbed Marjie's wrist and pulled her through the portal, along with the others.

The sensation of passing through was disorienting, a whirl of colours and sensations that felt both unnerving and oddly comforting.

They emerged on the beach, washing up on the shore like a pile of fish, still in their mermaid forms. The transition from the weightlessness of the ocean to the gravity of land was jarring, leaving them splayed out on the sand, gasping for breath.

Before they could process their abrupt return, Declan was there, rushing towards Delia.

The relief on his face was almost heartbreaking.

He cares. He really cares...He was in agony over the risk of losing me.

He helped her sit up, their eyes locking in a moment of shared understanding and relief. And then, their lips met in a kiss that spoke volumes, filled with the fear of what had almost been lost, and the joy of being reunited.

But the moment was fleeting. Declan pulled away, urgency replacing the softness in his eyes. "The Order, they're coming," he warned, his voice low and tense.

The news hit Delia like a wave of ice, snapping her back to reality. “The Order...”

Her mind flicked towards memories of her atrocious ex-husband and his betrayal, and the chaotic attacks she and the other Crones had faced in recent weeks, and Delia knew the danger was far from over.

52

MARJIE

Washed up on the beach, Marjie found herself in a surreal state of being – part mermaid, part human, and entirely overwhelmed by the events that had just unfolded. As she lay there, feeling the grains of sand against her scales, she caught sight of a familiar face.

Papa Jack rushed towards her, concern etched deeply into his features.

The sight of him, so steadfast and filled with worry, sent a wave of warmth through her, despite the oddity of her current form.

Her tail, once a magnificent blue, shimmered under the sun as it slowly began to transform back into legs, scales giving way to skin, the transition marking her return to the world she knew, her clothing reappearing in its place, blessedly dry.

The cold, damp sand began to cling to her skin, a gentle reminder of the earthy reality she had returned to. Papa Jack was there, right by her side, his eyes locked onto hers with a deep affection. The afternoon sun cast a warm glow around them, haloing him in light.

“Marjie, there’s something I’ve been meaning to tell you,” he said. “I tried to wait because I know you’ve been through so much, but today I thought I just might lose you.”

“Oh, don’t you worry about me,” Marjie chided him. “I’m fine, as always.”

“No, I felt it,” Papa Jack insisted. “You were in real danger. My heart ached to help you, but I feared there was nothing I could do...”

Marjie sighed softly. “Yes, I suppose we were in a pickle there, for a little while. You really felt that?”

Papa Jack nodded solemnly. "Marjie, I have to tell you," he started, his voice heavy with emotion, "I've held this in my heart for the longest time."

Marjie laughed, the sound light and bubbly. "Right now, Jack? While I'm still part fish?"

His laughter joined hers, easing the tension between them. "There's never a perfect time, is there? Especially not in Myrtlewood. But yes, now. I love you, Marjie. I've loved you since we first met. You light me up in a way I thought I'd never feel again."

"What do you say to a girl who's half a mermaid?" she quipped, still smiling.

"I say, 'I love you, whether you have legs or a tail.' I say, 'You've enchanted me, Marjie, completely'."

She paused, her smile lingering as she absorbed his words. "Give me a moment to catch my breath," she finally said.

Papa Jack's face fell slightly, mistaking her light-hearted response for hesitation. "I'm sorry, it's too soon, isn't it? After everything..."

"No, not at all," Marjie quickly reassured him, reaching out to touch his hand.

Marjie, still dizzy from their aquatic escapade, couldn't help but giggle at the absurdity of her situation. Here she was, half-mermaid on a beach, transitioning back to her human form, while the man she deeply admired declared his heart. It was like something out of a fantastical romance novel, yet it was real and happening to *her*.

Papa Jack, seeing her giggle, couldn't help but let out a small chuckle himself, though his was tinged with nervousness. "I must seem quite the fool, professing love like a love-struck youth while you're, well, changing forms," he said, his hand reaching out to gently brush a strand of wet hair from her face. His touch was tender, reverent almost, as if he were afraid she might vanish like seafoam.

"What do you say to that?" he asked again, his voice steadier now, but still thick with emotion. He waited, holding his breath for her response, his heart laid bare on the sandy shore.

Shaking her head, Marjie reached for his hand, squeezing it reassuringly. "It's not that, not at all, you silly goose. There's no need for you to tell me what I already know," she said, her tone soft but filled with conviction.

He looked puzzled for a moment, so she added, "And I hope you know that I feel the same. I might have been in the depths of the ocean, but my thoughts were with you."

Relief washed over Papa Jack's face, transforming it back into its usual warm joviality. He laughed, a sound of pure joy, as the tension of the moment broke like the waves behind them.

"Marjie," he said, his voice warm, the name itself a caress.

"Jack," she replied. The absurdity of their situation seemed to fade into the background as they sat there, arm in arm.

His eyes searched hers, looking for the truth in her words. "No one ever calls me Jack," he said. "I don't tend to like it when they try, but it sounds good coming from you."

Marjie continued, her voice steady and sure, "And I hope you understand the depth of my feeling for you too. I've seen wonders today, faced fears I never knew I had, and through it all, my thoughts kept returning to you."

Papa Jack helped her to her feet. Her clothing, mercifully, had reappeared, and it was miraculously dry thanks to the powerful magic of the potion.

As Marjie stood with Papa Jack's help, she caught sight of another familiar face.

"Rosemary!" Marjie beckoned her nearer.

Rosemary had clearly been hovering nearby with an expression of concern and curiosity. She must have come to help, and her presence brought another wave of relief to Marjie. Despite the oddity of her situation, seeing her good friend made her feel grounded and connected to her normal life once again.

Marjie couldn't help but grin as Rosemary approached. "Look at you, coming to the rescue as always," Marjie teased gently, reaching out to greet her.

"I didn't do anything much," Rosemary admitted. "But Papa Jack said you were in trouble and I couldn't just sit around making truffles!" Her eyes scanned Marjie for any sign of injury or undue stress. "Are you okay? What on earth happened out there?"

Marjie started to explain. "Well, we happened to get on the sea king's bad side—" But then she paused, catching sight of the tense faces of the others nearby. Realising that perhaps this was neither the time nor the place for such a fantastical story, she stopped herself. "Perhaps that's a story for another time," she said with an apologetic smile.

Rosemary nodded. "Of course, when you're ready. Just glad to see you're back on land and safe." Her gaze then shifted to Jack, and she added teasingly, "Seems like you've had quite a day!"

Marjie laughed, squeezing Jack's hand, feeling the solidity of his support. "Yes, it's been quite the day indeed," she said, her heart full of gratitude.

Rosemary winked. "You know I always enjoy a good beach drama, especially when it involves magic and mermaids. Just make sure the next time you decide to go swimming with mythical creatures, you send me an invite."

They shared a light-hearted laugh, before Marjie returned her attention to the others. "What is it?" she asked. "Why is everyone so worried?"

"The Order is coming," Delia said.

Marjie sighed. "Oh course they are," she said, catching Rosemary's eye. "Danger and intrigue in Myrtlewood. It must be Tuesday!"

53
THE SHEPHERD

The Shepherd's steed pounded across the shoreline, its hooves kicking up sand and spray as it charged forward. Behind him, the elite Order soldiers marched in perfect formation, their weapons at the ready.

The Shepherd now knew that underestimating the crones would be a fatal mistake. They were formidable opponents, each wielding ancient magic that had shaped and protected Myrtlewood for generations. He'd miscalculated their power already, too many times. He'd been guilty of hubris all these years as he watched closely over Delia – manipulating her life from their sham of a marriage bed. She'd always been strong-willed, but she was a woman, and he'd been mistaken in thinking her weak and stupid. He knew better now. It wasn't their weakness that made women the enemy of the almighty, it was their deviousness, their taint on the sanctity of life. Women must be reined in, and the power that pulsed deep within him now, threatening to overwhelm him, whispered to him of their wrongfulness and drove him further towards his grand mission of creating a better world under the guidance of the Almighty.

The coastal wind whipped at the Shepherd's face, carrying with it the scent of brine and the whispers of the Almighty that thrummed in his ears.

His eyes scanned the horizon, piercing the veil of the morning mist, searching for any sign of the enemy. Somewhere out there, they lurked, the ones who would willingly sabotage the plans of the Almighty, and he would not rest until they were vanquished.

The Rogue, elusive and reportedly hard to kill, was nothing but a minor inconvenience in the grand design, yet stamping him out was necessary to ensure the Order's control. There could be no loose ends.

The Shepherd smiled, slowly. "The Rogue will be eliminated, as will the entire Veiled Sisterhood," he whispered to himself, reaching momentarily towards the blade at his belt. "And the powers of the crones will become mine, in line with the will of the Almighty."

As he rode, the Shepherd's mind raced with visions of the power that would soon be his to command. The Crone magic, ancient and potent, would be the key to getting the upper hand against the Veiled Sisterhood and their horrendous moral plague, an important tool with which he would reshape the world in the image of the Almighty.

The Order's soldiers, handpicked for their loyalty and skill, awaited his command, ready to plunge into battle at his slightest nod.

The blade in his belt pulsed with eagerness, a reflection of his own unwavering resolve. It was enchanted, and he'd sought it out, with one goal in mind. *The Rogue must be neutralised.*

The beach stretched out before him, an endless expanse of sand and surf, the boundary between the known and the unknown. The soldiers riding behind him were but a reminder of the strength of his cause.

Suddenly, a flicker caught the Shepherd's eye, a shadow in the periphery of his vision. He reined in his steed, his senses heightened, every nerve in his body tingling with anticipation. The soldiers behind him halted, their weapons at the ready, poised for action at a moment's notice.

The Shepherd's gaze scanned the shoreline. The wind picked up, whipping the sand into a frenzy, the air charged with an electric tension. And then, for the briefest of moments, he saw it in the distance: a group of figures, huddled in the distance near the water's edge.

As he spurred his steed forward once more, the Shepherd's resolve hardened into an unbreakable diamond.

The Almighty's will would be done.

The stage was set, the players in motion, and the final act was about to begin.

54
DECLAN

Declan moved with purpose, his driftwood staff etching intricate patterns into the sand. The design was complex, and the swirls and lines subtly pulsed with magic which faded moments after he drew them. He could feel the power building, the very air crackling with energy.

Behind him, Delia and the other Crones – Agatha, Ingrid, and Marjie – were still recovering from their underwater adventure with Rosemary and Papa Jack supporting them. The winter sun shone on their faces as they savoured a moment of peace.

But Declan couldn't shake the growing sense of unease, the prickling at the back of his neck that warned of approaching danger. The Order was coming, their malevolent presence drawing near.

He finished the last major lines of the design, the pattern

almost complete. Then, with a sense of urgency, he rushed back to the group, his expression grim.

"It's time to go," he said, his voice brooking no argument. "The Order is almost here."

The Crones leapt to action. Well, Marjie and Delia did. Agatha groaned and grumbled, and Ingrid told her to focus, her weariness falling away as adrenaline kicked in. Declan wasted no time, casting a portal. The shimmering gateway opened, a doorway to safety, the centre of Myrtlewood visible on the other side.

"Quickly, through the portal!" Declan urged, guiding the group towards the rippling light.

Delia hung back, the last to approach, her eyes locked on Declan's. As she stepped into the portal, halfway through, realisation dawned on her face as Declan held his position several metres back. He wasn't following. He had to stay behind.

"Declan, no!" she cried, reaching for him. "Come with us!"

But Declan shook his head, a sad smile on his lips. "There's something I must do," he said softly. "I'm sorry, Delia."

He stepped forward to her and leaned in, his lips meeting hers in a kiss, passionate and intense, a goodbye and a promise all in one. Then, with gentle but firm hands, he pushed her through the portal.

Delia's cry of protest was cut off as the portal closed, sealing her safely in Myrtlewood. Declan turned back to the design in the sand, adding the final touches with swift, precise movements.

The thunder of hooves filled the air as the Order crested the dunes, their black horses kicking up sand. Declan straightened, his staff at the ready, as he faced the approaching threat alone.

Benedict rode at the head of the Order. Declan could feel the raw energy emanating from him, a twisted, corrupted force that made his skin crawl.

"Betrayer!" Benedict bellowed as he came to a halt, exactly where Declan had intended for him to be. "You dare defy the Order, defy the Almighty?"

Declan stood his ground, his gaze unwavering. "You're weak, Benedict," he retorted, his voice steady. "You're so afraid of losing control that you'll destroy anything that threatens your power."

Benedict's eyes blazed with dark power, a searing intensity that made Declan flinch. The power was immense, far greater than anything he had ever encountered.

“You may be hard to kill,” Benedict said slowly. “However, that will be your downfall. You've grown cocky in your misguided sense of immortality. This blade”—he drew a weapon, a small sword from an emerald studded sheath, brandishing it in the air—“is enchanted. It will cut through all your magical protections, whatever they be. This is the end for you.”

For a moment, Declan felt a flicker of fear, a primal terror that threatened to overwhelm him. But he pushed it down, his resolve hardening.

“I'm not afraid of a tiny weapon like that,” Declan said, deliberately taunting Benedict and slowly stepping back, leading the Order to trudge forward, just slightly, perfectly into place.

"You will pay for your insubordination, Rogue!" Benedict cried.

Declan allowed a smile to spread gleefully across his face.

"Is that so?" He tapped the staff on the final line and uttered the words that spoke to this land, that called forth the magical protections latent in the earth and activated his enchantment.

Serpell an gwrians, dybrians y'n bys

Declan jumped back as the symbols and patterns glowed where he'd carved them into the beach, and a brilliant light burst forth from the very earth itself, growing, expanding, until a massive portal opened.

"What have you done?" Benedict screamed.

"Just a little parting gift from me," said Declan.

With a roar of fury, the Crimson Shepherd hurled his enchanted blade through the air, its edge glinting with malevolent energy as it spun towards Declan. Too late – he tried to dodge, but the blade found its mark, embedding itself deep in his chest.

Pain exploded through his body, a searing agony that made him gasp for breath. He stumbled, his hand clutching at the wound, as the Order vanished into the portal which closed up, leaving Declan alone on the beach, grasping at the sword.

He collapsed onto the sand, the blade still lodged in his chest. Blood seeped through his fingers, staining the sand a violent red.

But even as the pain threatened to consume him, Declan's thoughts were of Delia. She was safe, and that was all that mattered.

55
DELIA

One moment Delia was standing on the beach, the salty sandy wind biting her skin, and the next she found herself in a graceless heap on the grassy circle in the middle of Myrtlewood. She blinked, disoriented, as she untangled her limbs from those of her fellow Crones.

"What the hell just happened?" she muttered, brushing grass and dirt from her jeans.

But even as the words left her mouth, the realisation hit her like a punch to the gut. Declan had stayed behind, facing the Order alone. The idiot had probably done something stupidly heroic, like sacrificing himself to save them.

Panic rose in her throat, bitter and sharp. She couldn't lose him.

"We have to go back," she said, her voice tight. "Declan's in trouble."

The other Crones, still dazed from their sudden teleportation, looked at her with confusion and concern. But they didn't argue. They knew the stakes and they understood the fierce pull of loyalty that came before even a rather strong craving for tea or sherry.

They raced through the streets of Myrtlewood, ignoring the startled looks from passing townsfolk. Delia's heart pounded in her ears, a relentless drumbeat of fear and adrenaline. *Please be okay. Please don't leave me.*

The beach came into view, the sand glinting in the sunlight. And there, lying motionless on the shore, was Declan. Delia's breath caught in her throat as she caught sight of the blade protruding from his chest, the metal glinting cruelly.

She sprinted towards him, sand flying beneath her feet. "Declan!" she cried, dropping to her knees beside him.

His face was pale, his breathing shallow. But his eyes fluttered open as she touched his cheek, and a weak smile curved his lips. "Hey, Fireball," he murmured.

"This is not the time for cute names," she snapped, tears blurring her vision. "What were you thinking, staying behind like that?! Where are the Order? Did Jerry do this to you?"

Fury blazed through her at the thought of her ex-husband.

"Had to keep you safe," Declan said, his voice barely above a whisper. "Don't worry, I'll be fine."

"How can I not worry?" Delia cried, her hands hovering over the blade, afraid to touch it. "You've got a freaking sword sticking out of your chest!"

Declan's hand closed over hers, his skin clammy. "You need to remove it," he said, his gaze intense despite the pain.

Marjie shook her head frantically. “That sounds like a terrible idea.”

“No...” Declan said. “It’s...it’s enchanted. Leaving it like this will do more damage. A simple blade I’d have pulled out myself, but this...I can’t. I need help.”

"No way,” said Delia. “If we just remove it you’ll bleed out."

The other Crones gathered around, their faces grim.

Agatha and Marjie bickered about the best approach, but Delia tuned them out, her eyes locked on Declan. Ingrid stepped forward, her eyes deep and searching. She stared long and hard at the injured rogue before speaking.

"He's right," she said softly. "Leaving it in will be worse."

Delia looked at her, torn. Every instinct screamed at her to leave the blade, to not risk making things worse. But the look in Ingrid’s eyes matched Declan's, the absolute certainty softening her resolve.

"Please, Delia," he whispered. "Trust me."

With shaking hands, Delia grasped the hilt of the blade. The other Crones held Declan steady, their faces taut with tension. Delia took a deep breath, uttering a silent plea to any gods that might be listening, and pulled.

The blade slid out with a sickening sound, and Declan arched, a strangled cry tearing from his throat. Delia tossed the blade aside, pressing her hands against the wound, waiting for the hot gush of blood.

But it never came.

Instead, beneath her palms, the wound began to knit itself back together. Skin and muscle and sinew, weaving back into wholeness as if by magic. Delia watched, her mouth agape, as the wound closed, leaving nothing but smooth, unmarked skin.

"How...?" she breathed, her mind reeling.

Declan sat up slowly, wincing. He caught Delia's hand, his fingers lacing with hers. "There's something I ought to tell you."

EPILOGUE

The evening settled over Delia's cottage like a cosy blanket, the crackling fire in the hearth chasing away the chill of the eventful day. Declan, still recovering from his ordeal, was wrapped up snugly on the sofa, a steaming mug of tea in his hands.

Marjie bustled about the kitchen, whipping up a batch of her famous hearty stew along with freshly baked bread, the scents of which filled the air, a balm to frayed nerves and weary souls.

Kitty, ever the attentive host, made sure everyone's glasses were topped up. She moved through the room with her usual flair, a tray of drinks balanced expertly in her hands.

Agatha, of course, was more than happy to partake. She settled into an armchair, a glass of whiskey in hand, her sharp eyes taking in the scene with amusement and exasperation.

Even Ingrid was there, perched on the edge of her seat as if ready to bolt at any moment. No one, least of all Ingrid herself, could quite comprehend what had possessed her to join this impromptu gathering. But there she was, a bemused expression on her face as she sipped her tea.

The conversation flowed gently. Laughter mingled with the crackling of the fire, and for a moment, all seemed right with the world.

Until Delia's phone rang.

She frowned, pulling the device from her pocket. The screen lit up with Gilly's name, and a flicker of worry crossed Delia's face. She excused herself, slipping into the kitchen for a bit of privacy.

"Hello, love," Delia said.

"Mum, I'm glad I've caught you..." Gilly's voice was tense, strained in a way that made Delia's heart clench.

"You sound tense. Are the kids okay?" Delia asked, her mind already racing with worst-case scenarios.

"The kids are fine," Gilly assured her. "But there's something I've got to tell you."

Delia paused. Not an hour ago, Declan had uttered almost those exact words, right before turning her world upside down with the revelation of his apparent immortality.

A wry smile tugged at her Delia's lips as she said, "Well then, you can join the line."

A personal message from Iris

Hello lovelies. Thank you so much for joining me and the

Myrtlewood Crones. If you enjoyed this book, please leave a rating or review to help other people find it!

You can preorder the The Crone of Arcane Cinders, next Myrtlewood Crones book in the series, on Kindle (paperbacks will be out close to the release date in January).

I'm also working on a 9th Myrtlewood Mysteries book, Impractical Magic!

If this is your first time reading my books, you might also want to check out the original Myrtlewood Mysteries series, starting with Accidental Magic.

If you're looking for more books set in the same world, you might want to take a look at my Dreamrealm Mysteries series too.

I absolutely love writing these books and sharing them with you. Feel free to join my reader list and follow me on social media to keep up to date with my witchy adventures.

Many blessings,

Iris xx

P.S. You can also subscribe to my Patreon account for extra Myrtlewood stories and new chapters of my books before they're published, as well as real magical content like meditations and spells, and access to my Myrtlewood Discord community. Subscribing supports my writing and other creative work!

For more information, see: www.patreon.com/IrisBeagle hole

ACKNOWLEDGMENTS

A big thank you to all my wonderful Patreon supporters, especially:

John Stephenson

Danielle Kinghorn

Ricky Manthey

Wingedjewels

Elizabeth

Rachel

and William Winnichuk

About the Author

Iris Beaglehole is many peculiar things, a writer, researcher, analyst, druid, witch, parent, and would-be astrologer. She loves tea, cats, herbs, and writing quirky characters.

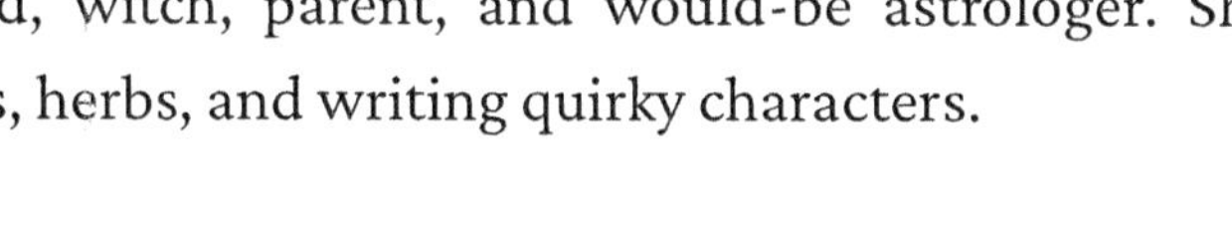

facebook.com/IrisBeaglehole
x.com/IrisBeaglehole
instagram.com/irisbeaglehole

Printed in Great Britain
by Amazon